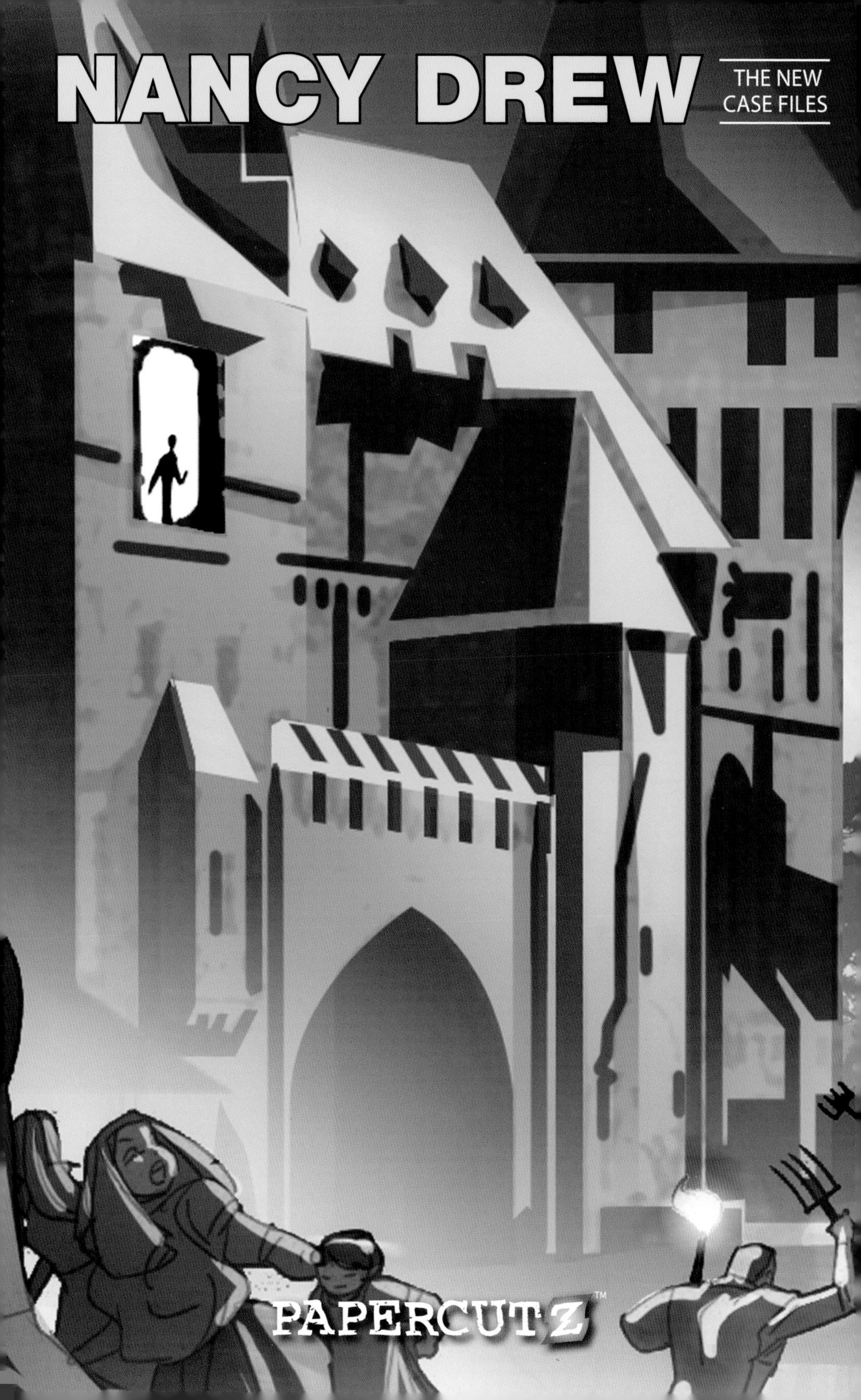
NANCY DREW
THE NEW CASE FILES
PAPERCUTZ

NANCY DREW GRAPHIC NOVELS AVAILABLE FROM PAPERCUTZ

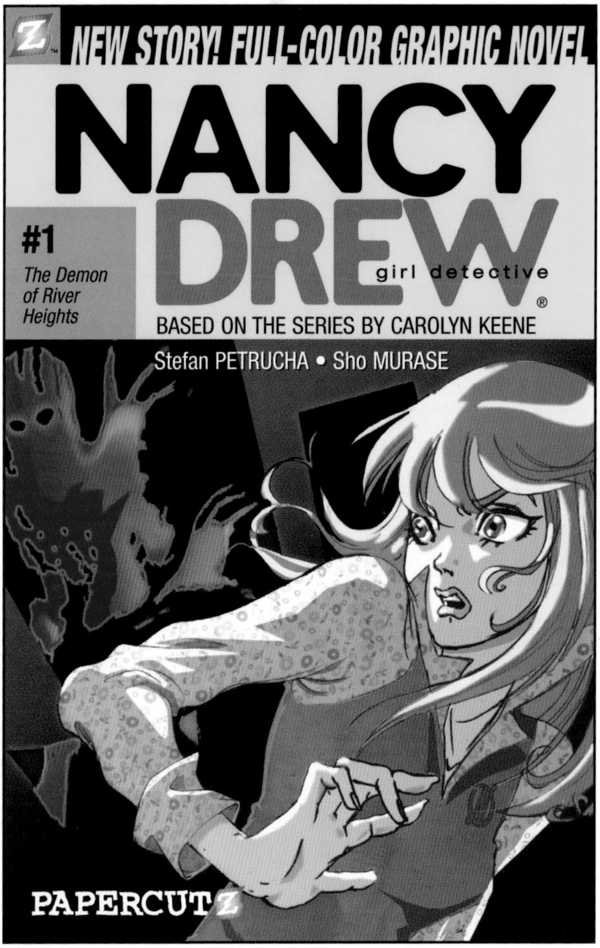

NEW STORY! FULL-COLOR GRAPHIC NOVEL
NANCY DREW
girl detective
#1
The Demon of River Heights
BASED ON THE SERIES BY CAROLYN KEENE
Stefan PETRUCHA • Sho MURASE
PAPERCUTZ

#1 "The Demon of River Heights"

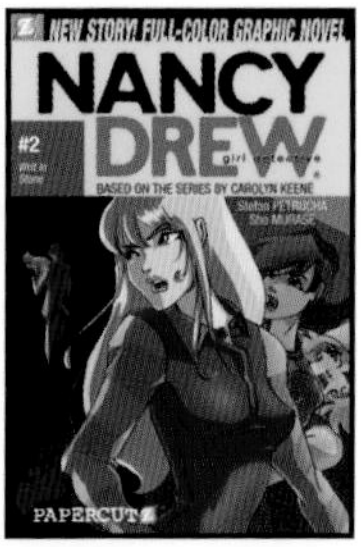

NANCY
DREW

#2 "Writ In Stone"

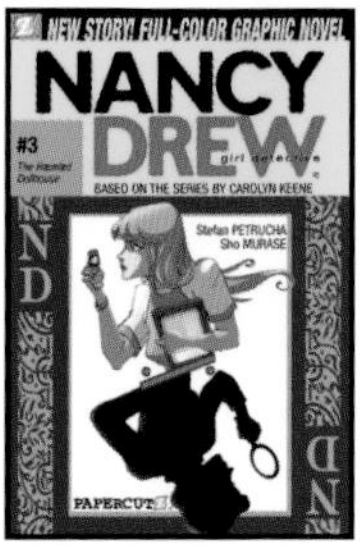

NEW STORY! FULL-COLOR GRAPHIC NOVEL
NANCY
DREW

#3 "The Haunted Dollhouse"

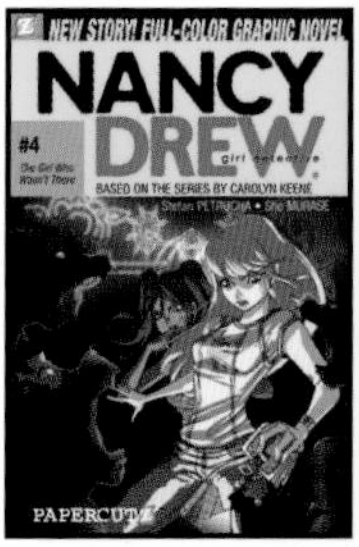

NEW STORY! FULL-COLOR GRAPHIC NOVEL
NANCY
DREW

#4 "The Girl Who Wasn't There"

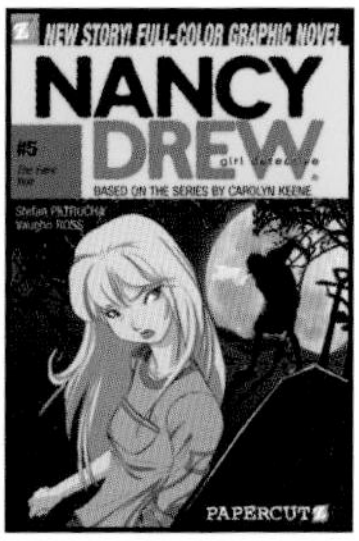

NEW STORY! FULL-COLOR GRAPHIC NOVEL
NANCY
DREW

#5 "The Fake Heir"

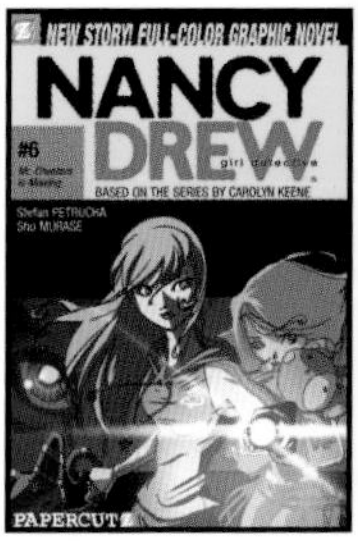

NEW STORY! FULL-COLOR GRAPHIC NOVEL
NANCY
DREW

#6 "Mr. Cheeters Is Missing"

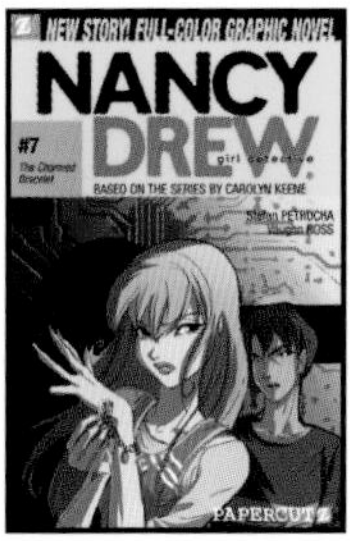

NEW STORY! FULL-COLOR GRAPHIC NOVEL
NANCY
DREW

#7 "The Charmed Bracelet"

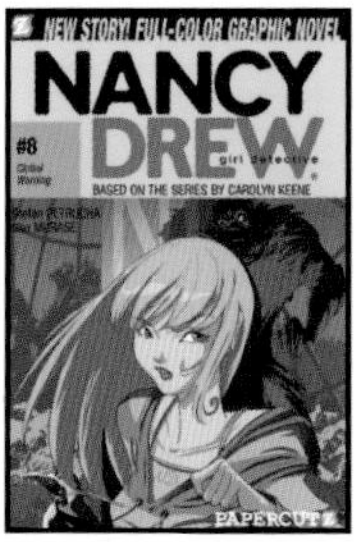

NEW STORY! FULL-COLOR GRAPHIC NOVEL
NANCY
DREW

#8 "Global Warning"

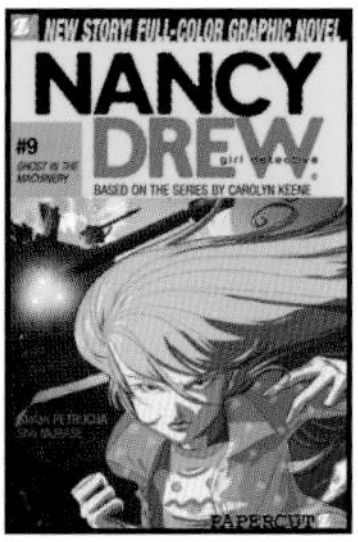

NEW STORY! FULL-COLOR GRAPHIC NOVEL
NANCY
DREW

#9 "Ghost In The Machinery"

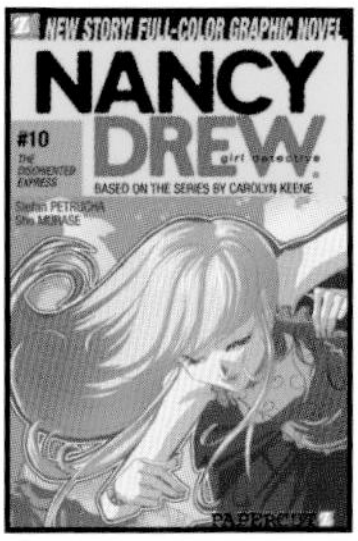

NEW STORY! FULL-COLOR GRAPHIC NOVEL
NANCY
DREW

#10 "The Disoriented Express"

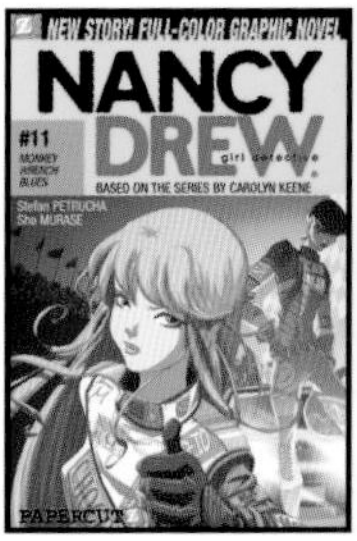

NEW STORY! FULL-COLOR GRAPHIC NOVEL
NANCY
DREW

#11 "Monkey Wrench Blues"

Graphic Novels are $7.95 in paperback, $12.95 hardcover. Please add $4.00 for postage and handling for the first book, add $1.00 for each additional book. Please make check payable to NBM Publishing. Send to:

Papercutz, 1200 County Rd. Rte. 523, Flemington, NJ 08822, 1-800-886-1223

www.papercutz.com

NANCY DREW
THE NEW CASE FILES

Girl Detective®

VAMPIRE SLAYER PART Two

STEFAN PETRUCHA & SARAH KINNEY • *Writers*
SHO MURASE • Artist
with 3D CG elements and color by CARLOS JOSE GUZMAN
Based on the series by
CAROLYN KEENE

New York

Let me introduce myself. I'm Nancy Drew. My friends call me Nancy. My enemies call me a lot of other things better left unsaid. See, I'm a detective. Not really. I mean, I don't have a license or anything. I don't carry a gun (not that I would touch one of those even if I could) or a badge. I'm not even old enough to have one. But I am old enough to know when something isn't right, when somebody's getting an unfair deal, or when someone's done something they shouldn't do. And I know how to stop them, catch them, and get them into the hands of the law, where they belong. I take those things seriously and I'm almost never wrong.

"Vampire Slayer" Part Two
STEFAN PETRUCHA & SARAH KINNEY – Writers
SHO MURASE — Artist
with 3D CG elements and color by CARLOS JOSE GUZMAN
BRYAN SENKA – Letterer
CHRIS NELSON & SHELLY STERNER – Production
MICHAEL PETRANEK – Associate Editor
JIM SALICRUP
Editor-in-Chief

ISBN: 978-1-59707-233-5 paperback edition
ISBN: 978-1-59707-234-2 hardcover edition

Printed in China.
September 2010 by Asia One Printing LTD.
13/F Asia One Tower
8 Fung Yip St., Chaiwan
Hong Kong

Distributed by Macmillan.

First Printing

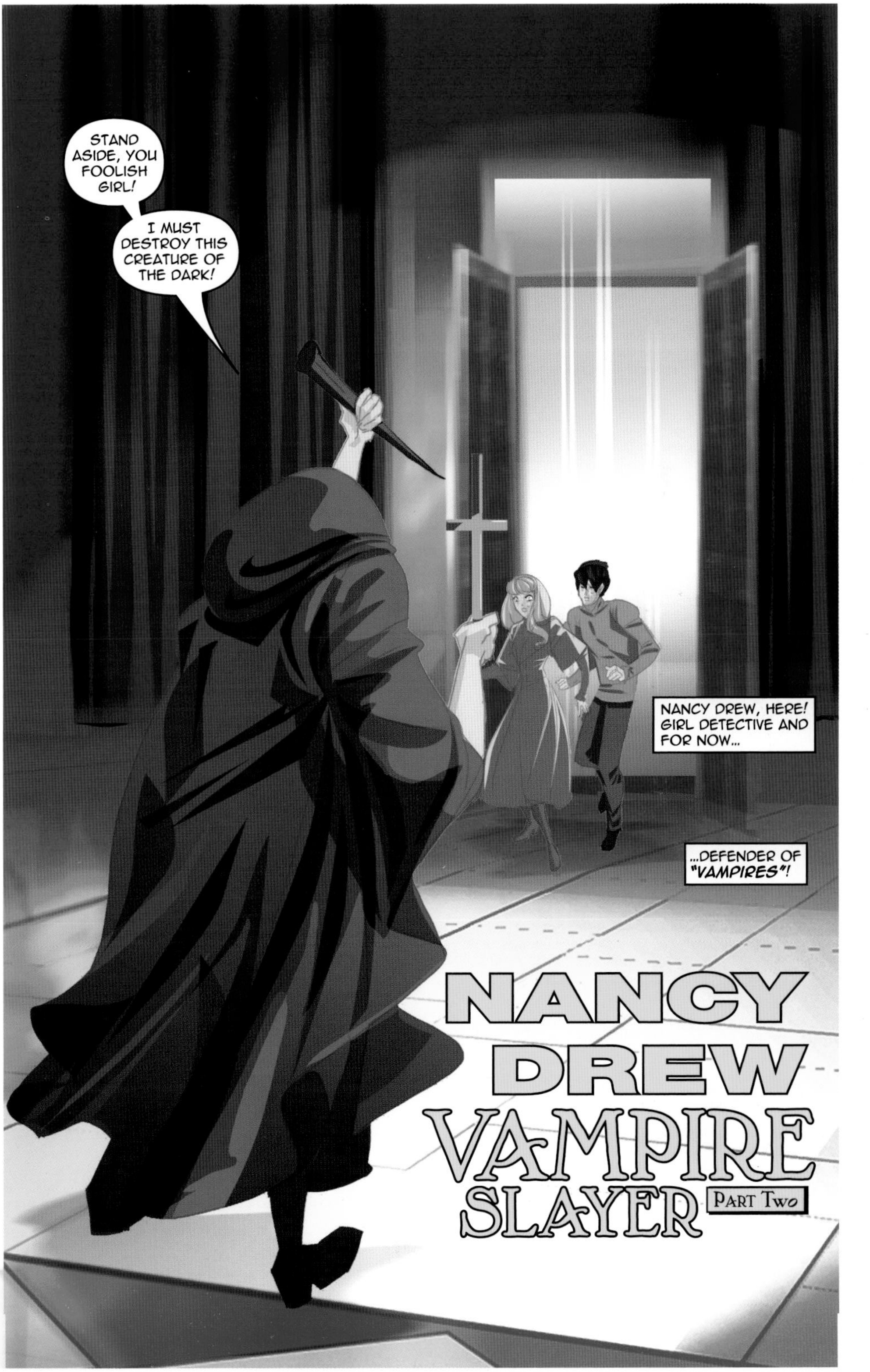
STAND ASIDE, YOU FOOLISH GIRL!
I MUST DESTROY THIS CREATURE OF THE DARK!
NANCY DREW, HERE! GIRL DETECTIVE AND FOR NOW...
...DEFENDER OF "VAMPIRES"!
NANCY DREW
VAMPIRE SLAYER
PART TWO

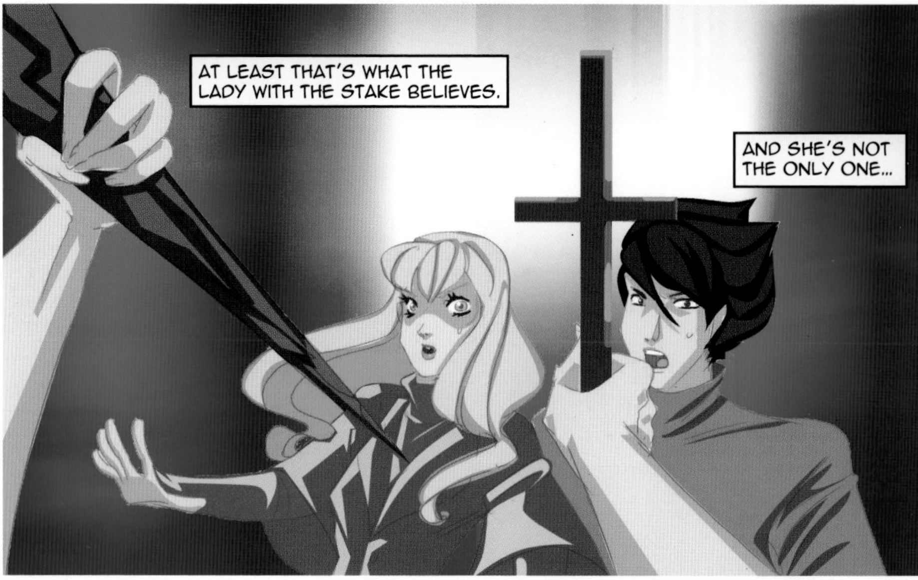
AT LEAST THAT'S WHAT THE LADY WITH THE STAKE BELIEVES.
AND SHE'S NOT THE ONLY ONE...

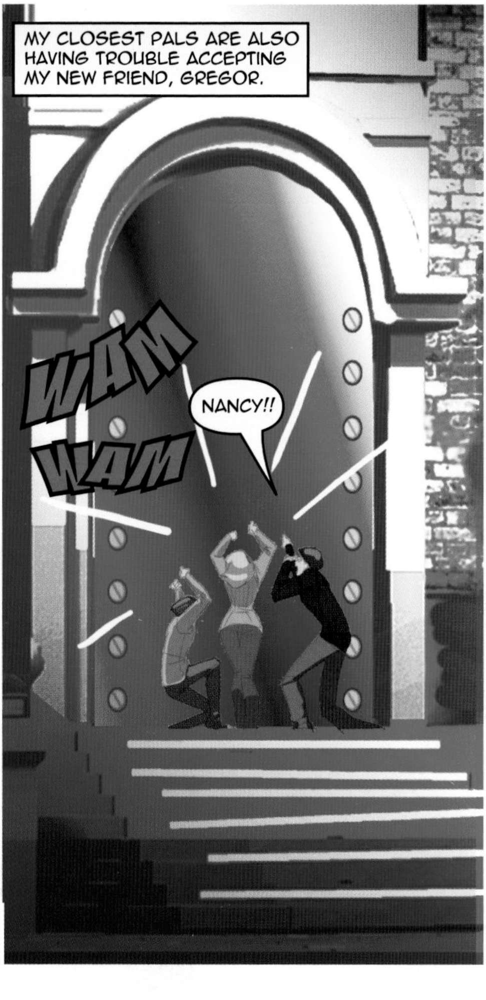
MY CLOSEST PALS ARE ALSO HAVING TROUBLE ACCEPTING MY NEW FRIEND, GREGOR.
WAM
WAM
NANCY!!

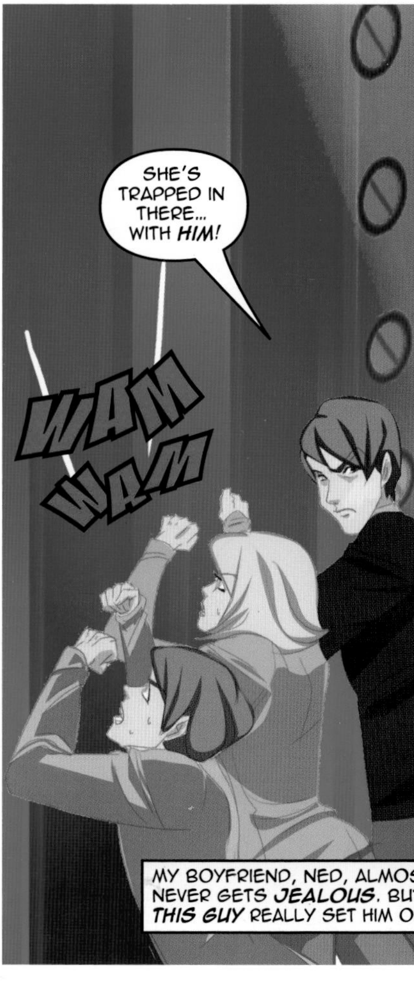
SHE'S TRAPPED IN THERE... WITH *HIM*!
WAM
WAM
MY BOYFRIEND, NED, ALMOST NEVER GETS *JEALOUS*. BUT, *THIS GUY* REALLY SET HIM OFF.

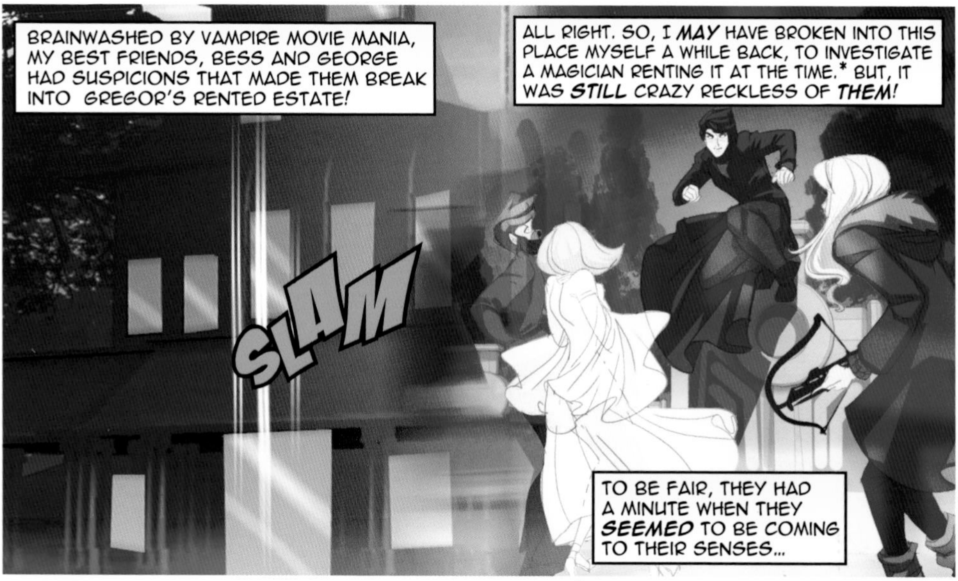
BRAINWASHED BY VAMPIRE MOVIE MANIA, MY BEST FRIENDS, BESS AND GEORGE HAD SUSPICIONS THAT MADE THEM BREAK INTO GREGOR'S RENTED ESTATE!
SLAM
ALL RIGHT. SO, I MAY HAVE BROKEN INTO THIS PLACE MYSELF A WHILE BACK, TO INVESTIGATE A MAGICIAN RENTING IT AT THE TIME.* BUT, IT WAS STILL CRAZY RECKLESS OF THEM!
TO BE FAIR, THEY HAD A MINUTE WHEN THEY SEEMED TO BE COMING TO THEIR SENSES...

*SEE NANCY DREW GRAPHIC NOVEL #14 "SLEIGHT OF DAN."

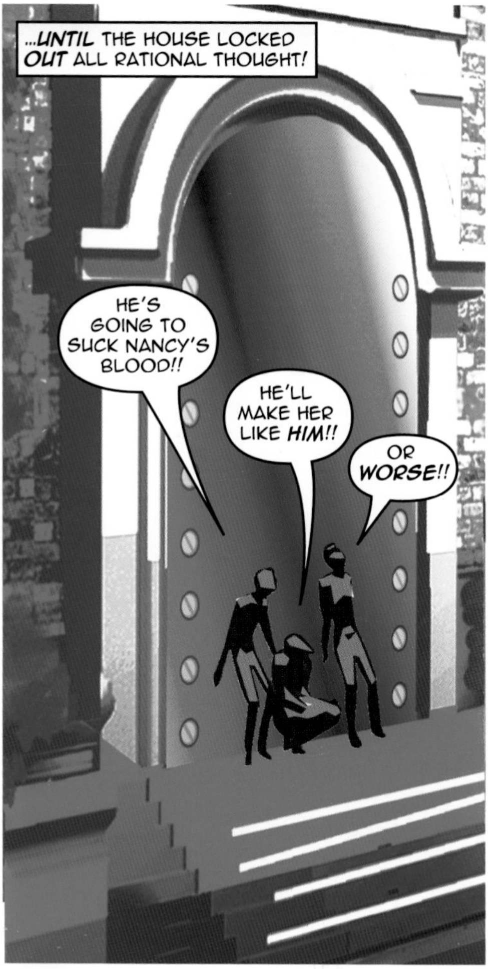
...UNTIL THE HOUSE LOCKED OUT ALL RATIONAL THOUGHT!
HE'S GOING TO SUCK NANCY'S BLOOD!!
HE'LL MAKE HER LIKE HIM!!
OR WORSE!!

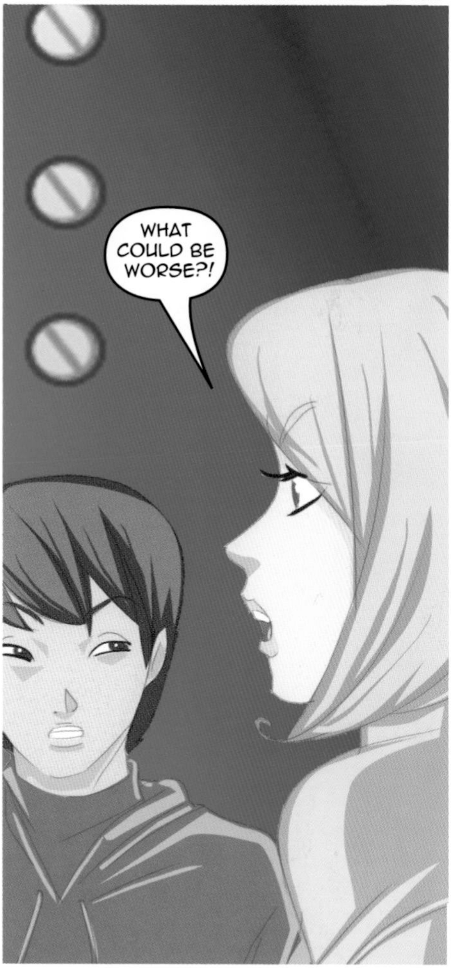
WHAT COULD BE WORSE?!

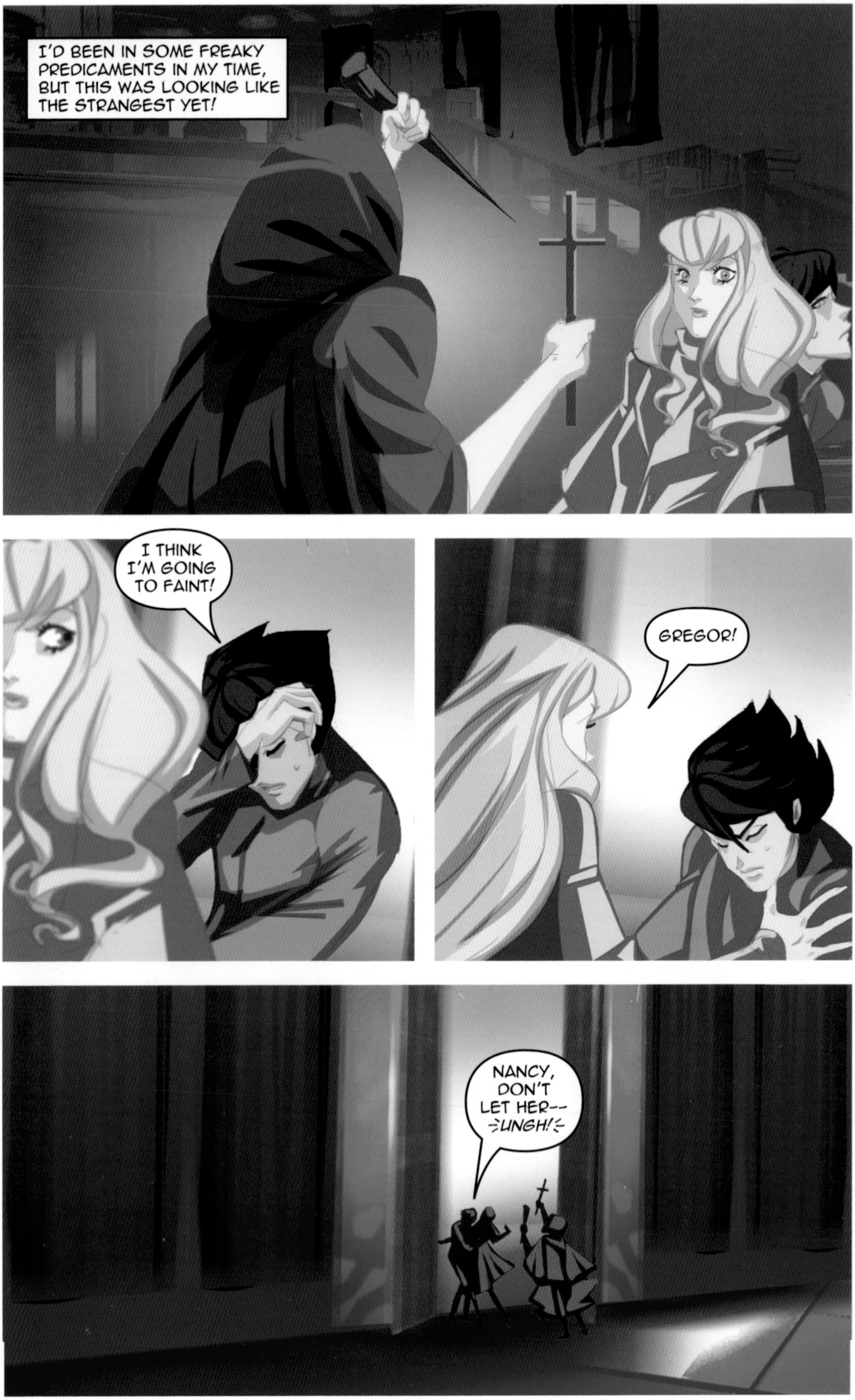

I'D BEEN IN SOME FREAKY PREDICAMENTS IN MY TIME, BUT THIS WAS LOOKING LIKE THE STRANGEST YET!
I THINK I'M GOING TO FAINT!
GREGOR!
NANCY, DON'T LET HER-- UNGH!

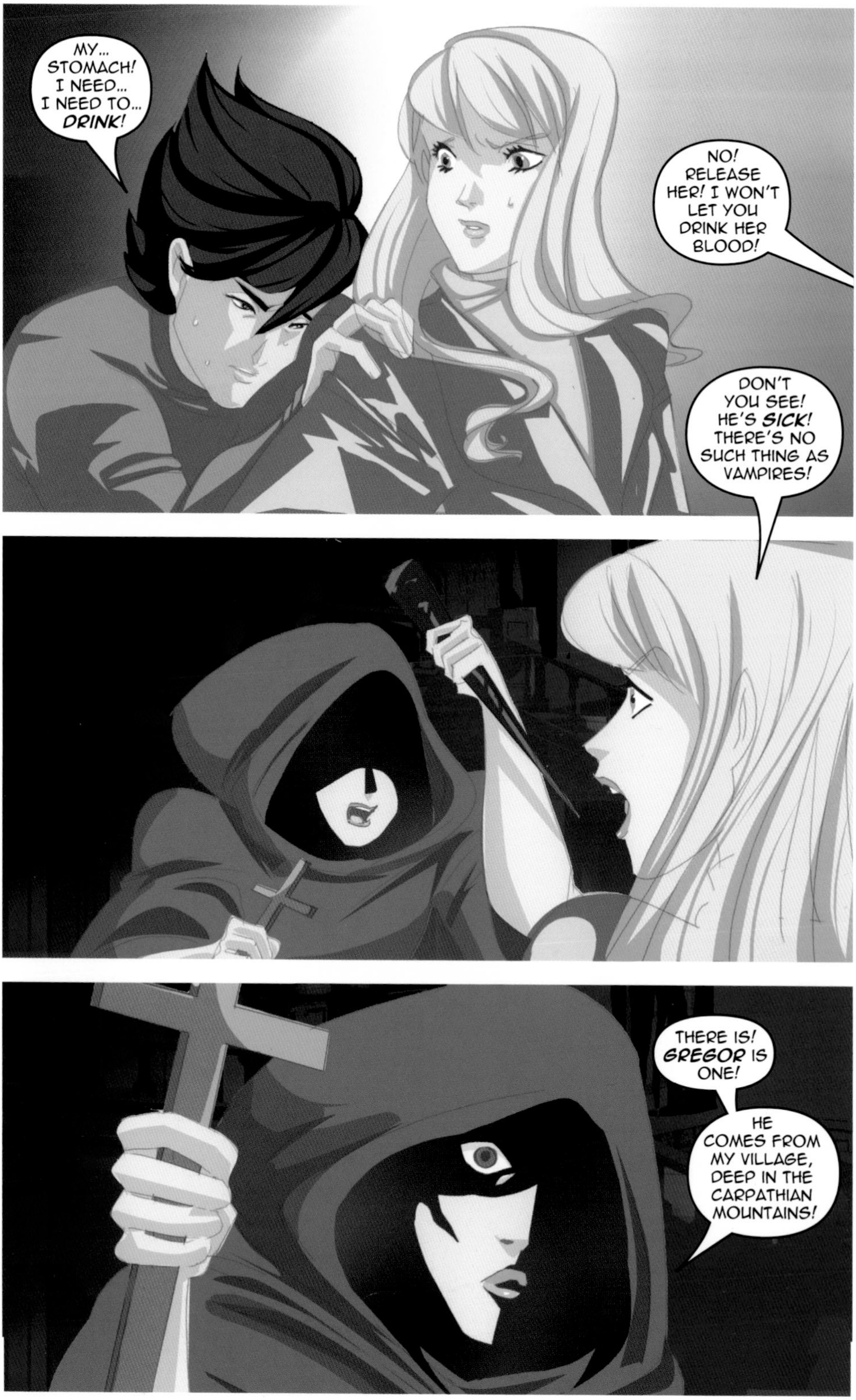
MY... STOMACH! I NEED... I NEED TO... DRINK!
NO! RELEASE HER! I WON'T LET YOU DRINK HER BLOOD!
DON'T YOU SEE! HE'S SICK! THERE'S NO SUCH THING AS VAMPIRES!
THERE IS! GREGOR IS ONE!
HE COMES FROM MY VILLAGE, DEEP IN THE CARPATHIAN MOUNTAINS!

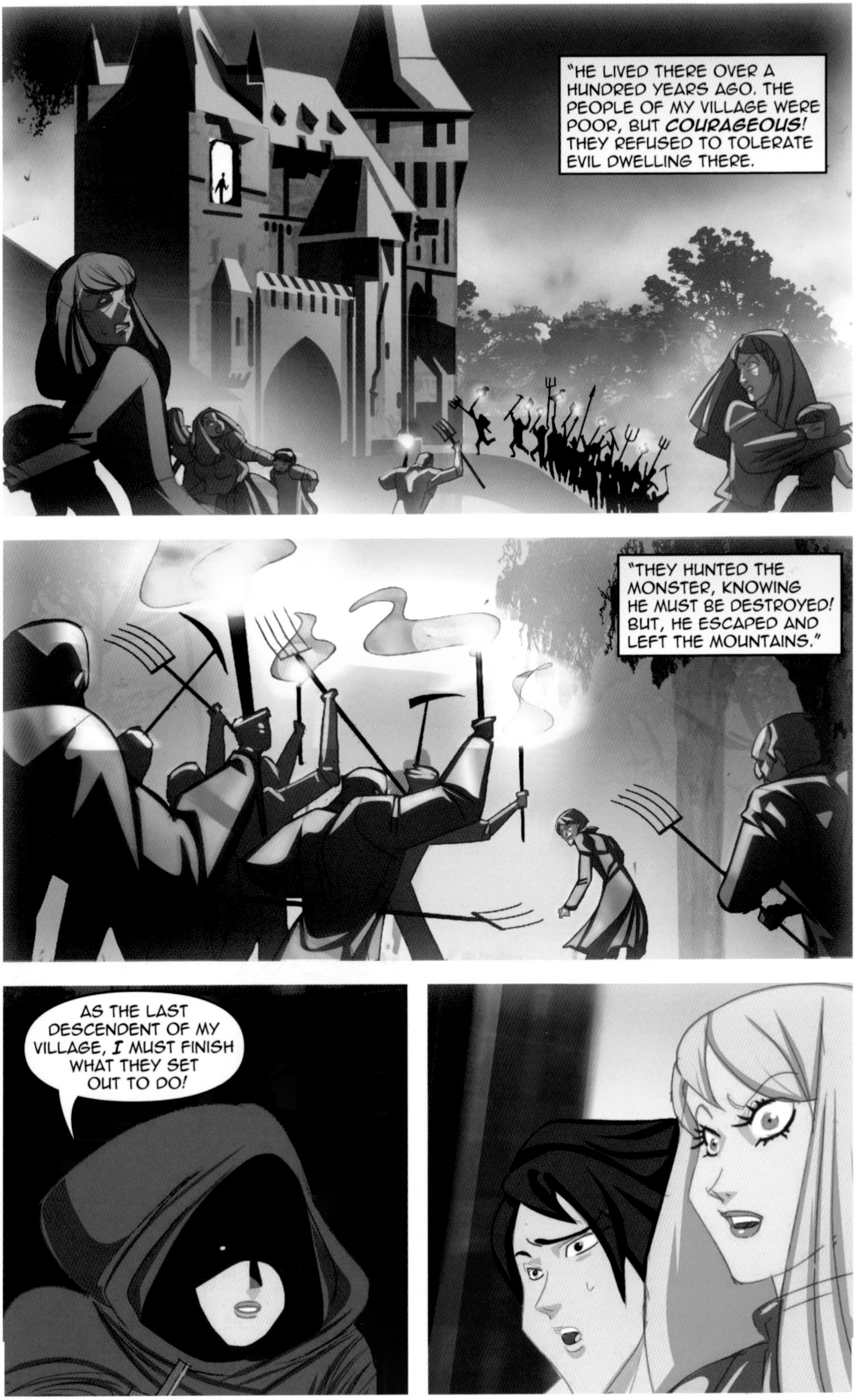
"HE LIVED THERE OVER A HUNDRED YEARS AGO. THE PEOPLE OF MY VILLAGE WERE POOR, BUT *COURAGEOUS!* THEY REFUSED TO TOLERATE EVIL DWELLING THERE.
"THEY HUNTED THE MONSTER, KNOWING HE MUST BE DESTROYED! BUT, HE ESCAPED AND LEFT THE MOUNTAINS."
AS THE LAST DESCENDENT OF MY VILLAGE, *I* MUST FINISH WHAT THEY SET OUT TO DO!

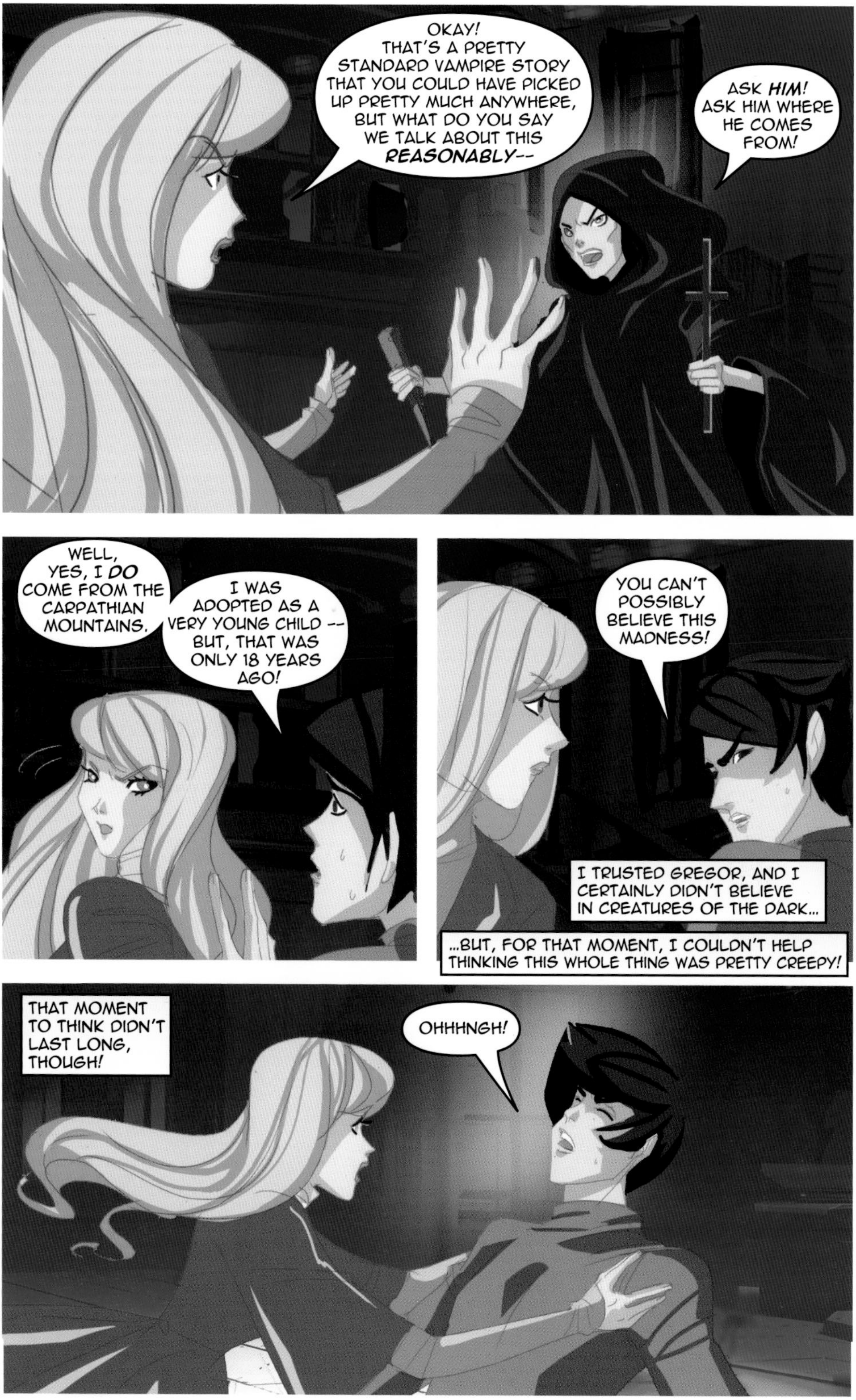
OKAY! THAT'S A PRETTY STANDARD VAMPIRE STORY THAT YOU COULD HAVE PICKED UP PRETTY MUCH ANYWHERE, BUT WHAT DO YOU SAY WE TALK ABOUT THIS *REASONABLY*--
ASK *HIM*! ASK HIM WHERE HE COMES FROM!
WELL, YES, I *DO* COME FROM THE CARPATHIAN MOUNTAINS.
I WAS ADOPTED AS A VERY YOUNG CHILD -- BUT, THAT WAS ONLY 18 YEARS AGO!
YOU CAN'T POSSIBLY BELIEVE THIS MADNESS!
I TRUSTED GREGOR, AND I CERTAINLY DIDN'T BELIEVE IN CREATURES OF THE DARK...
...BUT, FOR THAT MOMENT, I COULDN'T HELP THINKING THIS WHOLE THING WAS PRETTY CREEPY!
THAT MOMENT TO THINK DIDN'T LAST LONG, THOUGH!
OHHHNGH!

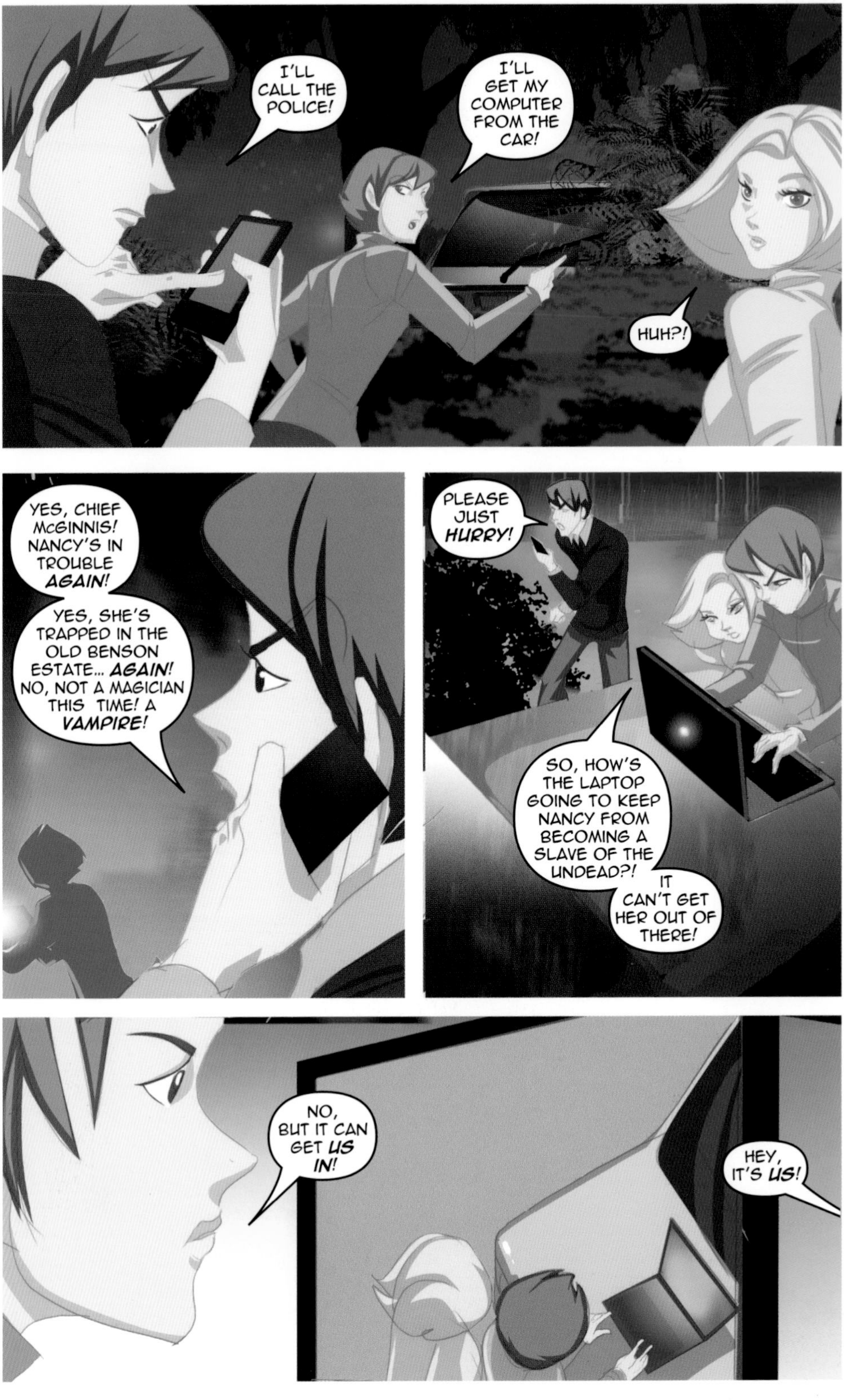
I'LL CALL THE POLICE!
I'LL GET MY COMPUTER FROM THE CAR!
HUH?!
YES, CHIEF McGINNIS! NANCY'S IN TROUBLE *AGAIN*!
YES, SHE'S TRAPPED IN THE OLD BENSON ESTATE... *AGAIN*! NO, NOT A MAGICIAN THIS TIME! A *VAMPIRE*!
PLEASE JUST *HURRY*!
SO, HOW'S THE LAPTOP GOING TO KEEP NANCY FROM BECOMING A SLAVE OF THE UNDEAD?!
IT CAN'T GET HER OUT OF THERE!
NO, BUT IT CAN GET *US IN*!
HEY, IT'S *US*!

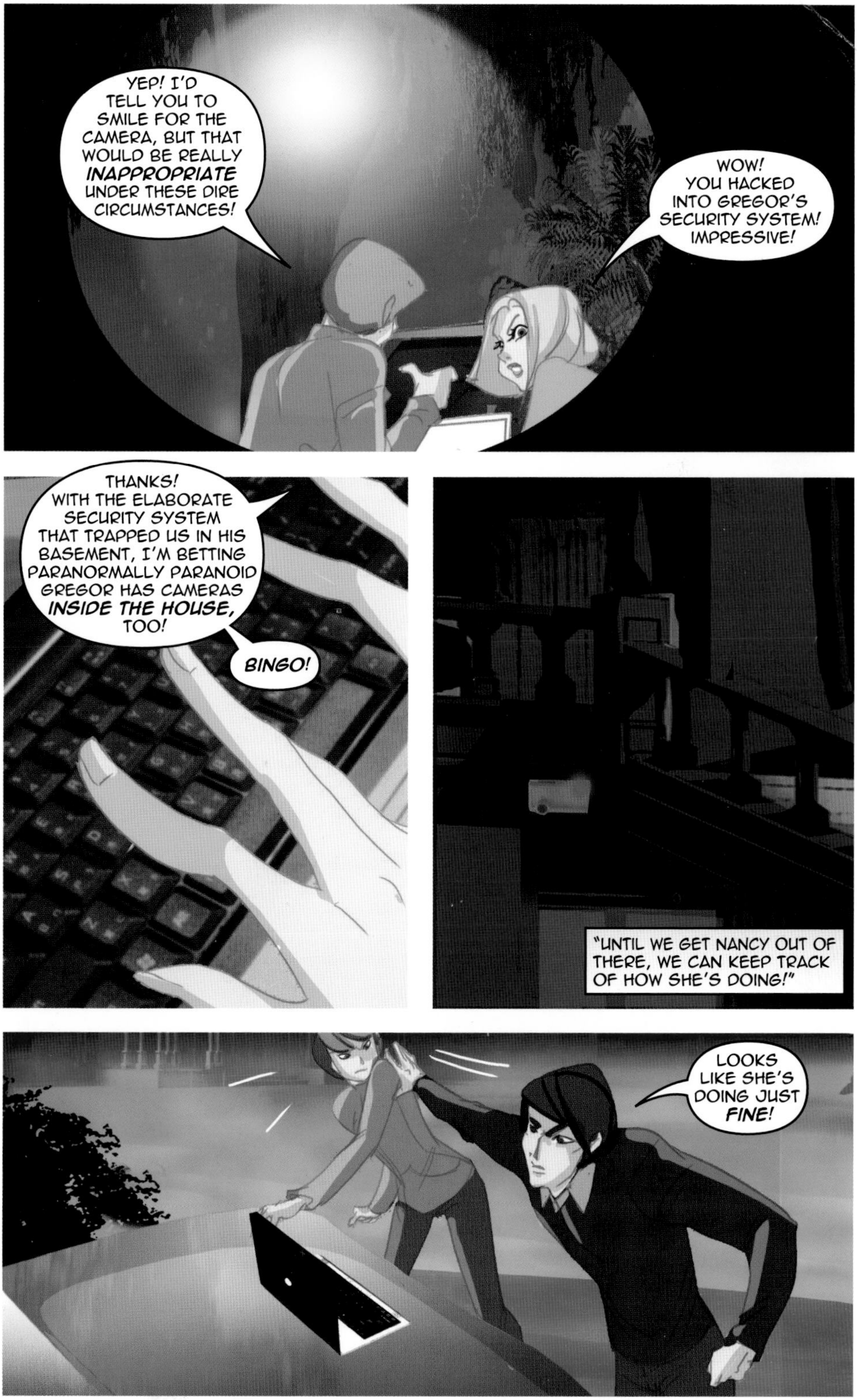
YEP! I'D TELL YOU TO SMILE FOR THE CAMERA, BUT THAT WOULD BE REALLY *INAPPROPRIATE* UNDER THESE DIRE CIRCUMSTANCES!
WOW! YOU HACKED INTO GREGOR'S SECURITY SYSTEM! IMPRESSIVE!
THANKS! WITH THE ELABORATE SECURITY SYSTEM THAT TRAPPED US IN HIS BASEMENT, I'M BETTING PARANORMALLY PARANOID GREGOR HAS CAMERAS *INSIDE THE HOUSE,* TOO!
BINGO!
"UNTIL WE GET NANCY OUT OF THERE, WE CAN KEEP TRACK OF HOW SHE'S DOING!"
LOOKS LIKE SHE'S DOING JUST *FINE!*

IT REALLY *WASN'T* MY BEST ANGLE!

SINCE I HAD NEVER BEEN ABLE TO TELL THEM GREGOR'S SECRET, MY PALS WERE TOTALLY CLUELESS.

NEW IN TOWN, GREGOR HAD SEEMED DESPERATE FOR MY HELP. BUT HE WAS TOO MISTRUSTFUL TO COME OUT AND TELL ME HIS SECRET PROBLEM.

HOW DO YOU SOLVE A MYSTERY THAT'S... WELL, A *TOTAL MYSTERY*?!

WE MET OFTEN, ALWAYS *AFTER SUNSET*. I COULD TELL HE WAS SUFFERING.

AFTER GETTING PRETTY CLOSE TO GREGOR...

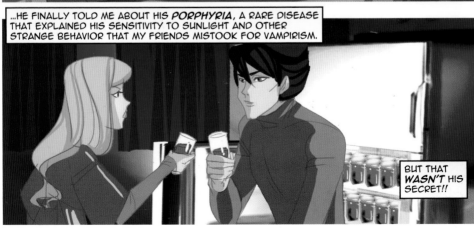

...HE FINALLY TOLD ME ABOUT HIS *PORPHYRIA*, A RARE DISEASE THAT EXPLAINED HIS SENSITIVITY TO SUNLIGHT AND OTHER STRANGE BEHAVIOR THAT MY FRIENDS MISTOOK FOR VAMPIRISM.

BUT THAT *WASN'T* HIS SECRET!!

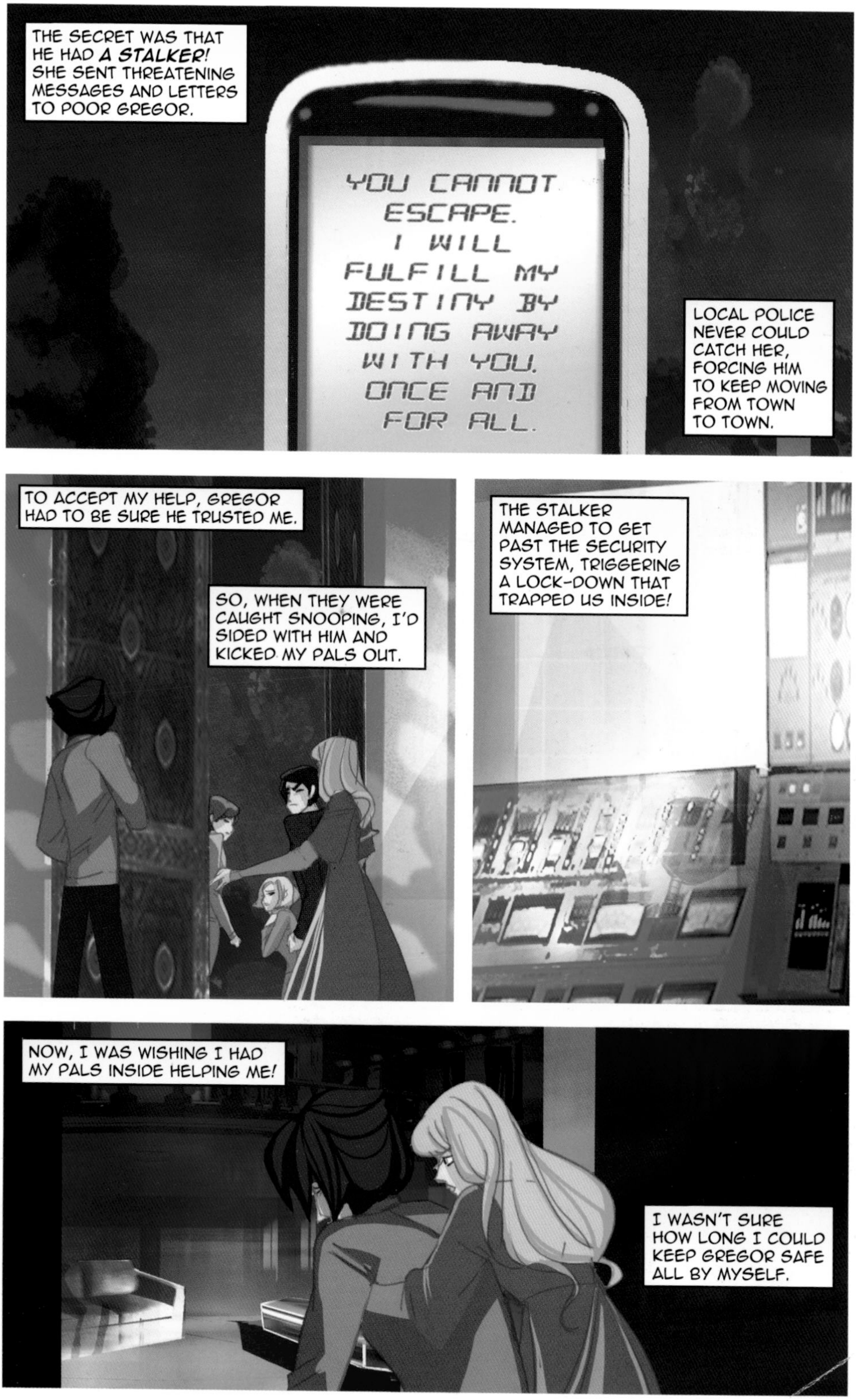
THE SECRET WAS THAT HE HAD A STALKER! SHE SENT THREATENING MESSAGES AND LETTERS TO POOR GREGOR.
YOU CANNOT ESCAPE. I WILL FULFILL MY DESTINY BY DOING AWAY WITH YOU. ONCE AND FOR ALL.
LOCAL POLICE NEVER COULD CATCH HER, FORCING HIM TO KEEP MOVING FROM TOWN TO TOWN.
TO ACCEPT MY HELP, GREGOR HAD TO BE SURE HE TRUSTED ME.
SO, WHEN THEY WERE CAUGHT SNOOPING, I'D SIDED WITH HIM AND KICKED MY PALS OUT.
THE STALKER MANAGED TO GET PAST THE SECURITY SYSTEM, TRIGGERING A LOCK-DOWN THAT TRAPPED US INSIDE!
NOW, I WAS WISHING I HAD MY PALS INSIDE HELPING ME!
I WASN'T SURE HOW LONG I COULD KEEP GREGOR SAFE ALL BY MYSELF.

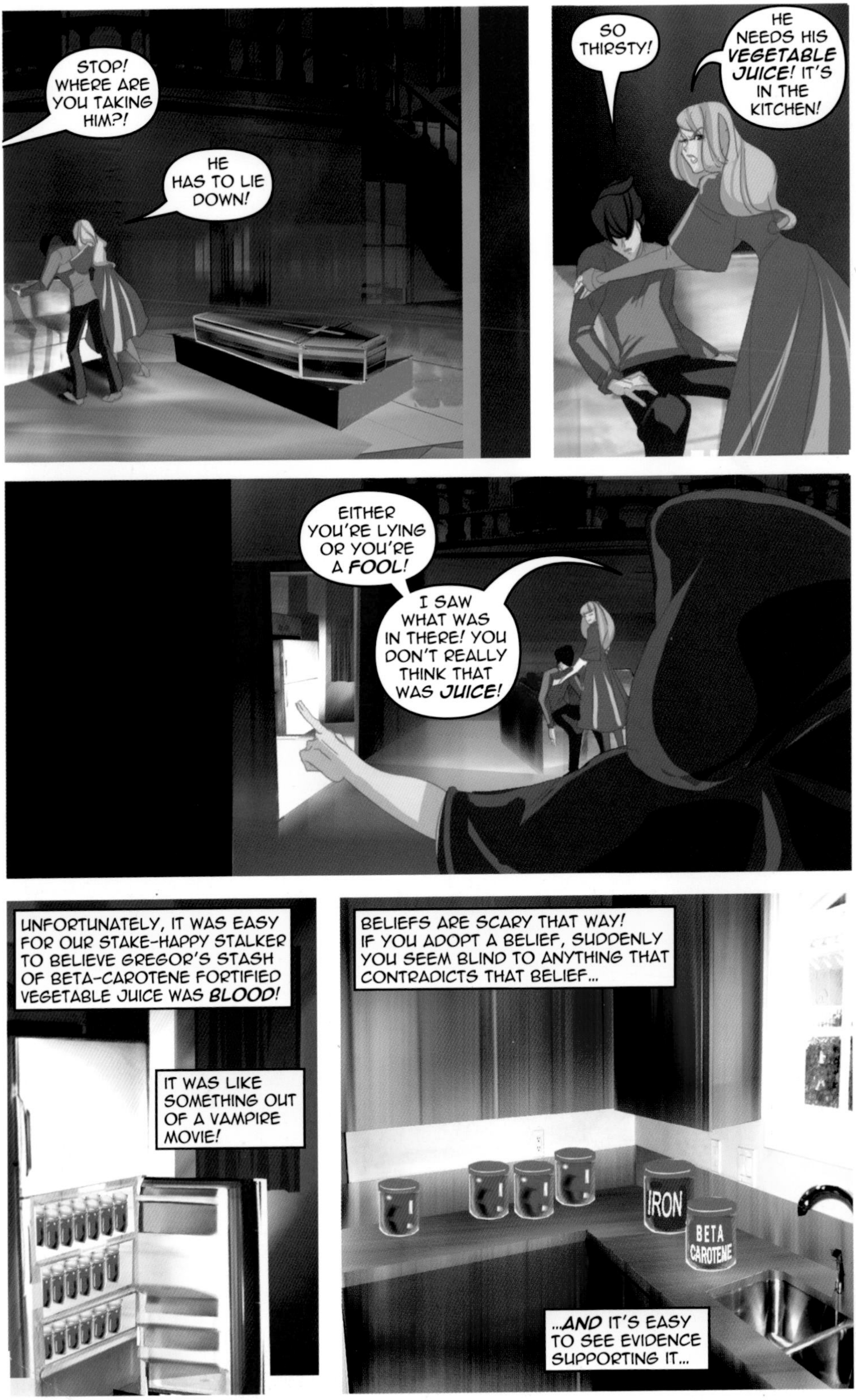
STOP! WHERE ARE YOU TAKING HIM?!
HE HAS TO LIE DOWN!
SO THIRSTY!
HE NEEDS HIS VEGETABLE JUICE! IT'S IN THE KITCHEN!
EITHER YOU'RE LYING OR YOU'RE A FOOL!
I SAW WHAT WAS IN THERE! YOU DON'T REALLY THINK THAT WAS JUICE!
UNFORTUNATELY, IT WAS EASY FOR OUR STAKE-HAPPY STALKER TO BELIEVE GREGOR'S STASH OF BETA-CAROTENE FORTIFIED VEGETABLE JUICE WAS BLOOD!
IT WAS LIKE SOMETHING OUT OF A VAMPIRE MOVIE!
BELIEFS ARE SCARY THAT WAY! IF YOU ADOPT A BELIEF, SUDDENLY YOU SEEM BLIND TO ANYTHING THAT CONTRADICTS THAT BELIEF...
IRON
BETA CAROTENE
...AND IT'S EASY TO SEE EVIDENCE SUPPORTING IT...

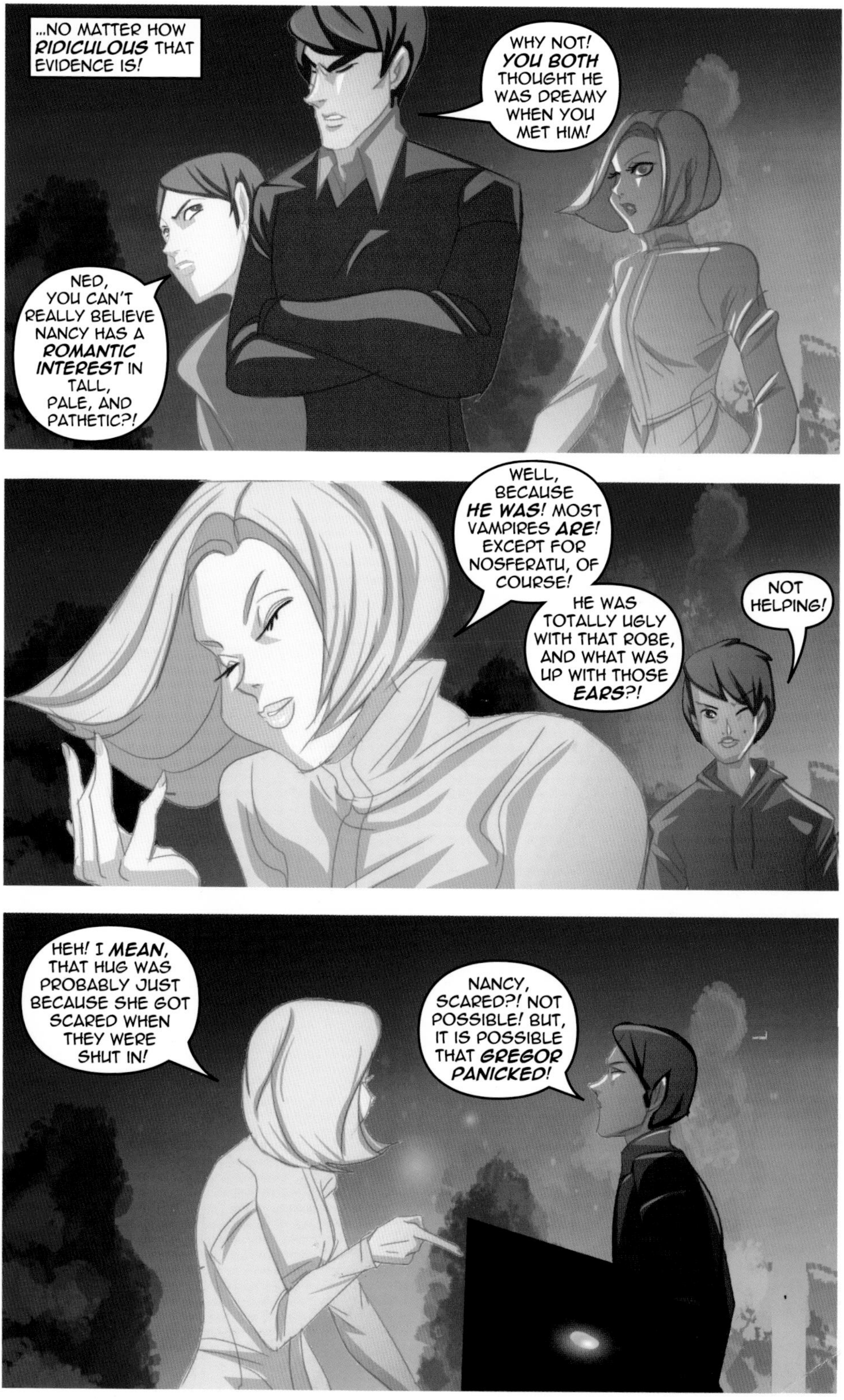
...NO MATTER HOW RIDICULOUS THAT EVIDENCE IS!
WHY NOT! YOU BOTH THOUGHT HE WAS DREAMY WHEN YOU MET HIM!
NED, YOU CAN'T REALLY BELIEVE NANCY HAS A ROMANTIC INTEREST IN TALL, PALE, AND PATHETIC?!
WELL, BECAUSE HE WAS! MOST VAMPIRES ARE! EXCEPT FOR NOSFERATU, OF COURSE!
HE WAS TOTALLY UGLY WITH THAT ROBE, AND WHAT WAS UP WITH THOSE EARS?!
NOT HELPING!
HEH! I MEAN, THAT HUG WAS PROBABLY JUST BECAUSE SHE GOT SCARED WHEN THEY WERE SHUT IN!
NANCY, SCARED?! NOT POSSIBLE! BUT, IT IS POSSIBLE THAT GREGOR PANICKED!

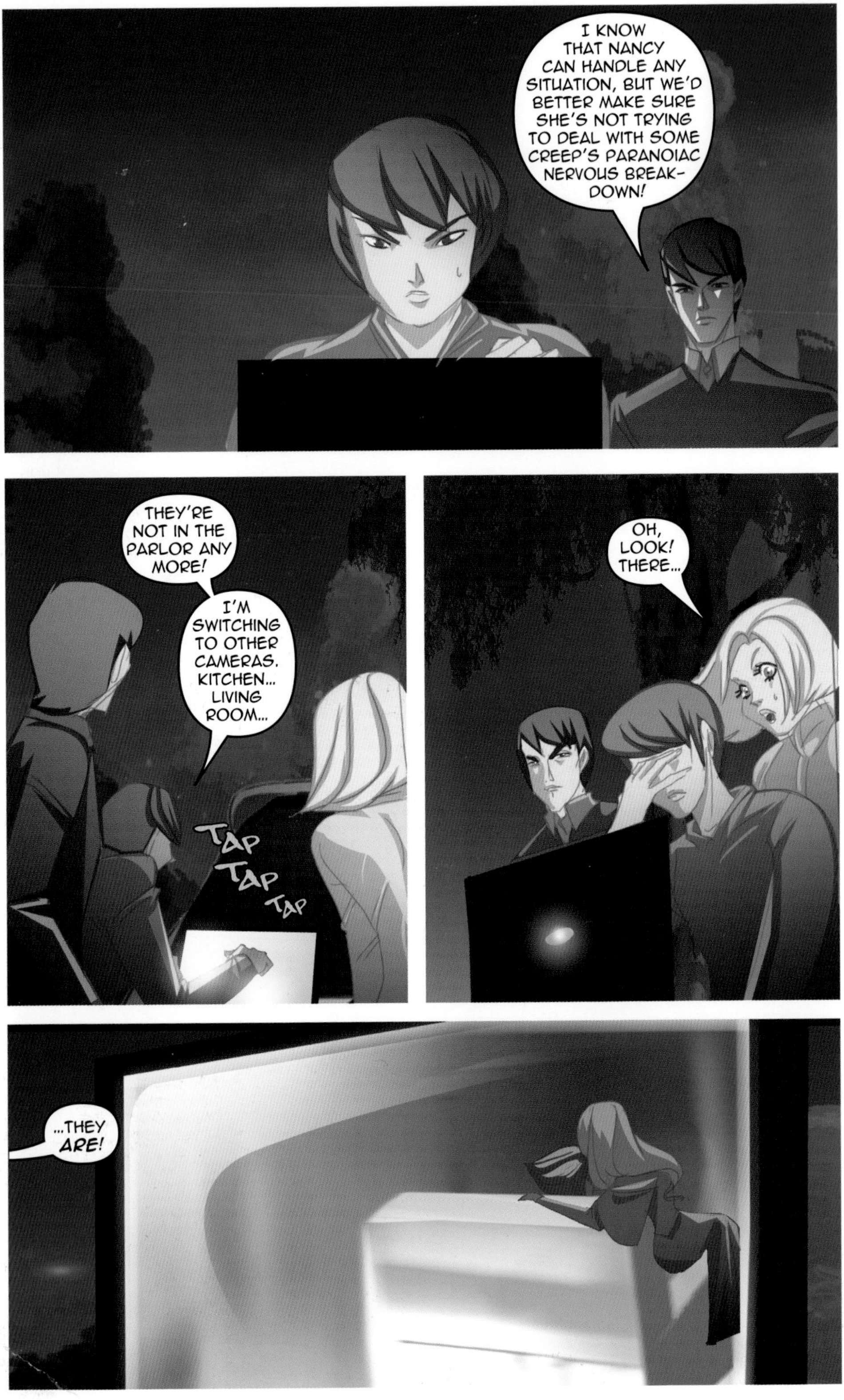
I KNOW THAT NANCY CAN HANDLE ANY SITUATION, BUT WE'D BETTER MAKE SURE SHE'S NOT TRYING TO DEAL WITH SOME CREEP'S PARANOIAC NERVOUS BREAK-DOWN!
THEY'RE NOT IN THE PARLOR ANY MORE!
I'M SWITCHING TO OTHER CAMERAS. KITCHEN... LIVING ROOM...
TAP TAP TAP
OH, LOOK! THERE...
...THEY ARE!

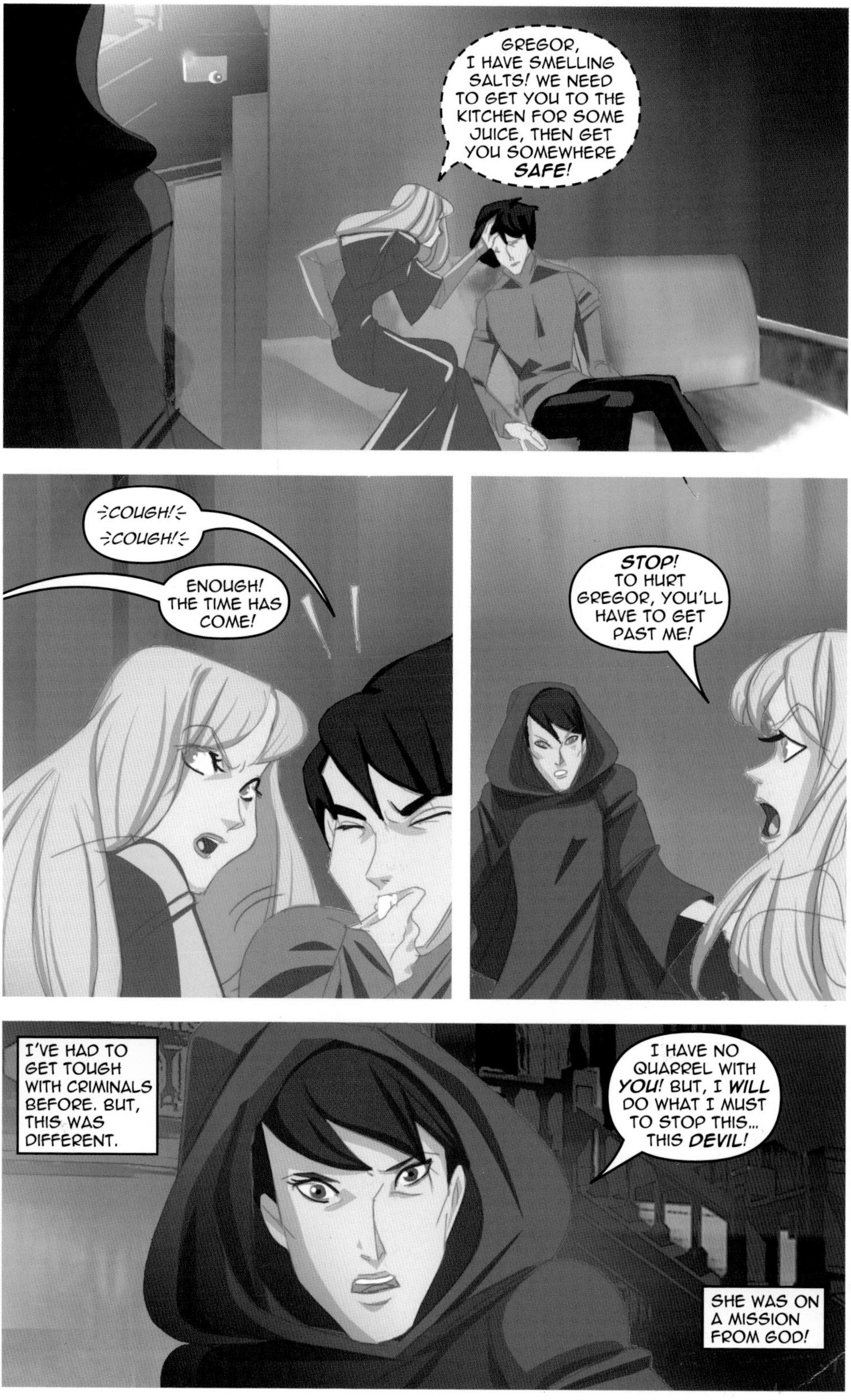
GREGOR, I HAVE SMELLING SALTS! WE NEED TO GET YOU TO THE KITCHEN FOR SOME JUICE, THEN GET YOU SOMEWHERE SAFE!
COUGH! COUGH!
ENOUGH! THE TIME HAS COME!
STOP! TO HURT GREGOR, YOU'LL HAVE TO GET PAST ME!
I'VE HAD TO GET TOUGH WITH CRIMINALS BEFORE. BUT, THIS WAS DIFFERENT.
I HAVE NO QUARREL WITH YOU! BUT, I WILL DO WHAT I MUST TO STOP THIS... THIS DEVIL!
SHE WAS ON A MISSION FROM GOD!

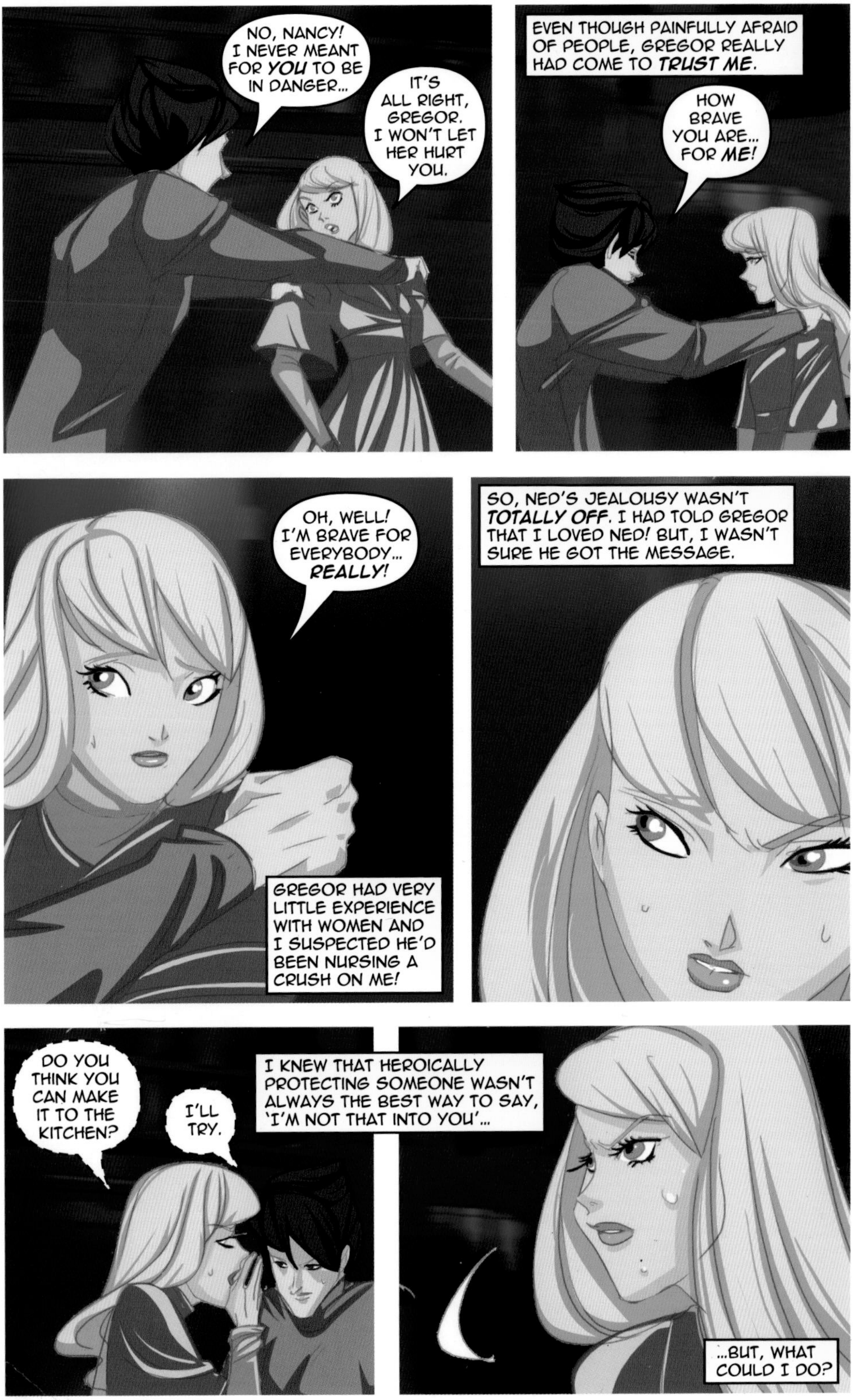
NO, NANCY! I NEVER MEANT FOR YOU TO BE IN DANGER...
IT'S ALL RIGHT, GREGOR. I WON'T LET HER HURT YOU.
EVEN THOUGH PAINFULLY AFRAID OF PEOPLE, GREGOR REALLY HAD COME TO TRUST ME.
HOW BRAVE YOU ARE... FOR ME!
OH, WELL! I'M BRAVE FOR EVERYBODY... REALLY!
GREGOR HAD VERY LITTLE EXPERIENCE WITH WOMEN AND I SUSPECTED HE'D BEEN NURSING A CRUSH ON ME!
SO, NED'S JEALOUSY WASN'T TOTALLY OFF. I HAD TOLD GREGOR THAT I LOVED NED! BUT, I WASN'T SURE HE GOT THE MESSAGE.
DO YOU THINK YOU CAN MAKE IT TO THE KITCHEN?
I'LL TRY.
I KNEW THAT HEROICALLY PROTECTING SOMEONE WASN'T ALWAYS THE BEST WAY TO SAY, 'I'M NOT THAT INTO YOU'...
...BUT, WHAT COULD I DO?

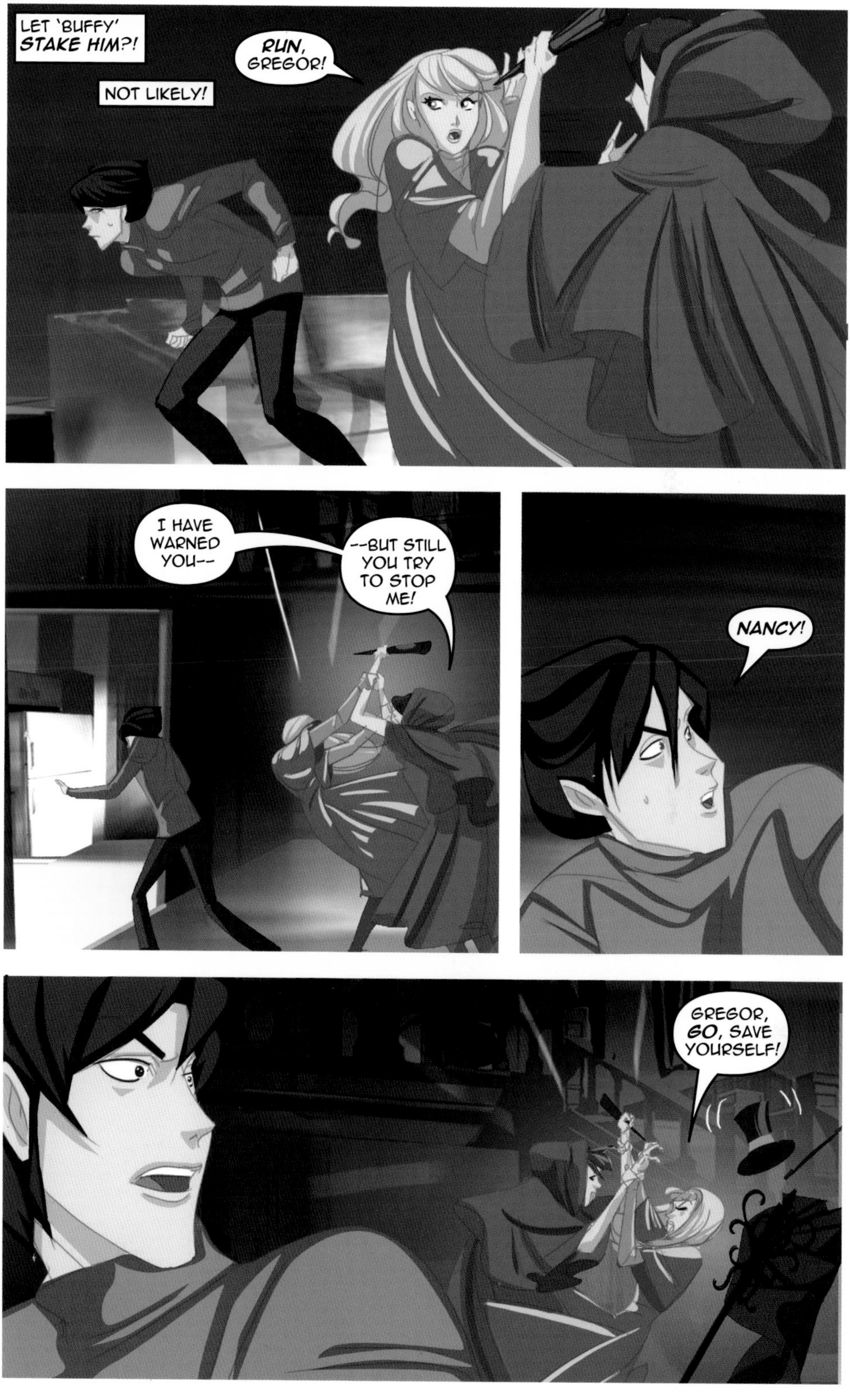
LET 'BUFFY' STAKE HIM?!
NOT LIKELY!
RUN, GREGOR!
I HAVE WARNED YOU--
--BUT STILL YOU TRY TO STOP ME!
NANCY!
GREGOR, GO, SAVE YOURSELF!

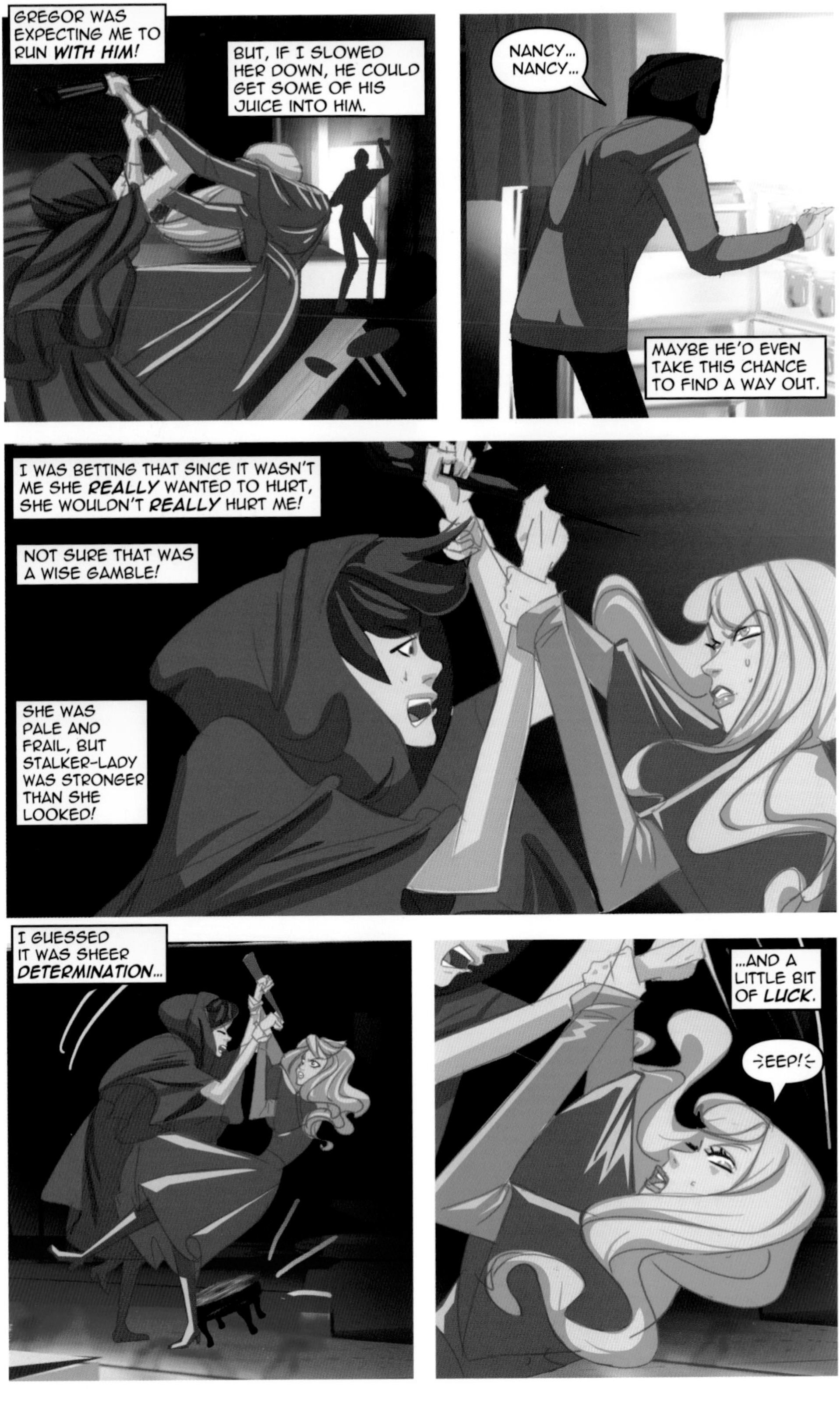
GREGOR WAS EXPECTING ME TO RUN WITH HIM!
BUT, IF I SLOWED HER DOWN, HE COULD GET SOME OF HIS JUICE INTO HIM.
NANCY... NANCY...
MAYBE HE'D EVEN TAKE THIS CHANCE TO FIND A WAY OUT.
I WAS BETTING THAT SINCE IT WASN'T ME SHE REALLY WANTED TO HURT, SHE WOULDN'T REALLY HURT ME!
NOT SURE THAT WAS A WISE GAMBLE!
SHE WAS PALE AND FRAIL, BUT STALKER-LADY WAS STRONGER THAN SHE LOOKED!
I GUESSED IT WAS SHEER DETERMINATION...
...AND A LITTLE BIT OF LUCK.
EEP!

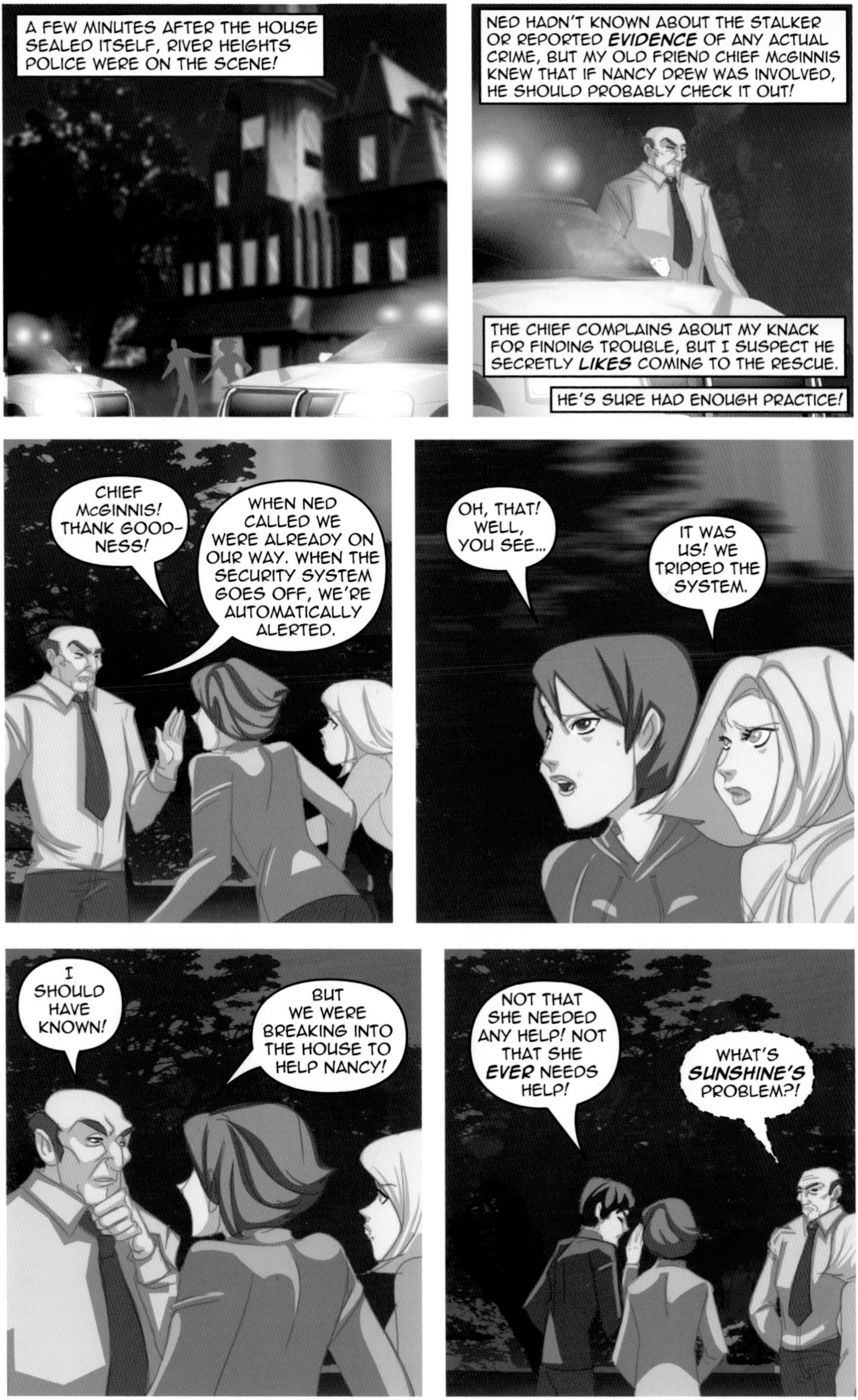
A FEW MINUTES AFTER THE HOUSE SEALED ITSELF, RIVER HEIGHTS POLICE WERE ON THE SCENE!
NED HADN'T KNOWN ABOUT THE STALKER OR REPORTED **EVIDENCE** OF ANY ACTUAL CRIME, BUT MY OLD FRIEND CHIEF McGINNIS KNEW THAT IF NANCY DREW WAS INVOLVED, HE SHOULD PROBABLY CHECK IT OUT!
THE CHIEF COMPLAINS ABOUT MY KNACK FOR FINDING TROUBLE, BUT I SUSPECT HE SECRETLY **LIKES** COMING TO THE RESCUE.
HE'S SURE HAD ENOUGH PRACTICE!
CHIEF McGINNIS! THANK GOODNESS!
WHEN NED CALLED WE WERE ALREADY ON OUR WAY. WHEN THE SECURITY SYSTEM GOES OFF, WE'RE AUTOMATICALLY ALERTED.
OH, THAT! WELL, YOU SEE...
IT WAS US! WE TRIPPED THE SYSTEM.
I SHOULD HAVE KNOWN!
BUT WE WERE BREAKING INTO THE HOUSE TO HELP NANCY!
NOT THAT SHE NEEDED ANY HELP! NOT THAT SHE **EVER** NEEDS HELP!
WHAT'S **SUNSHINE'S** PROBLEM?!

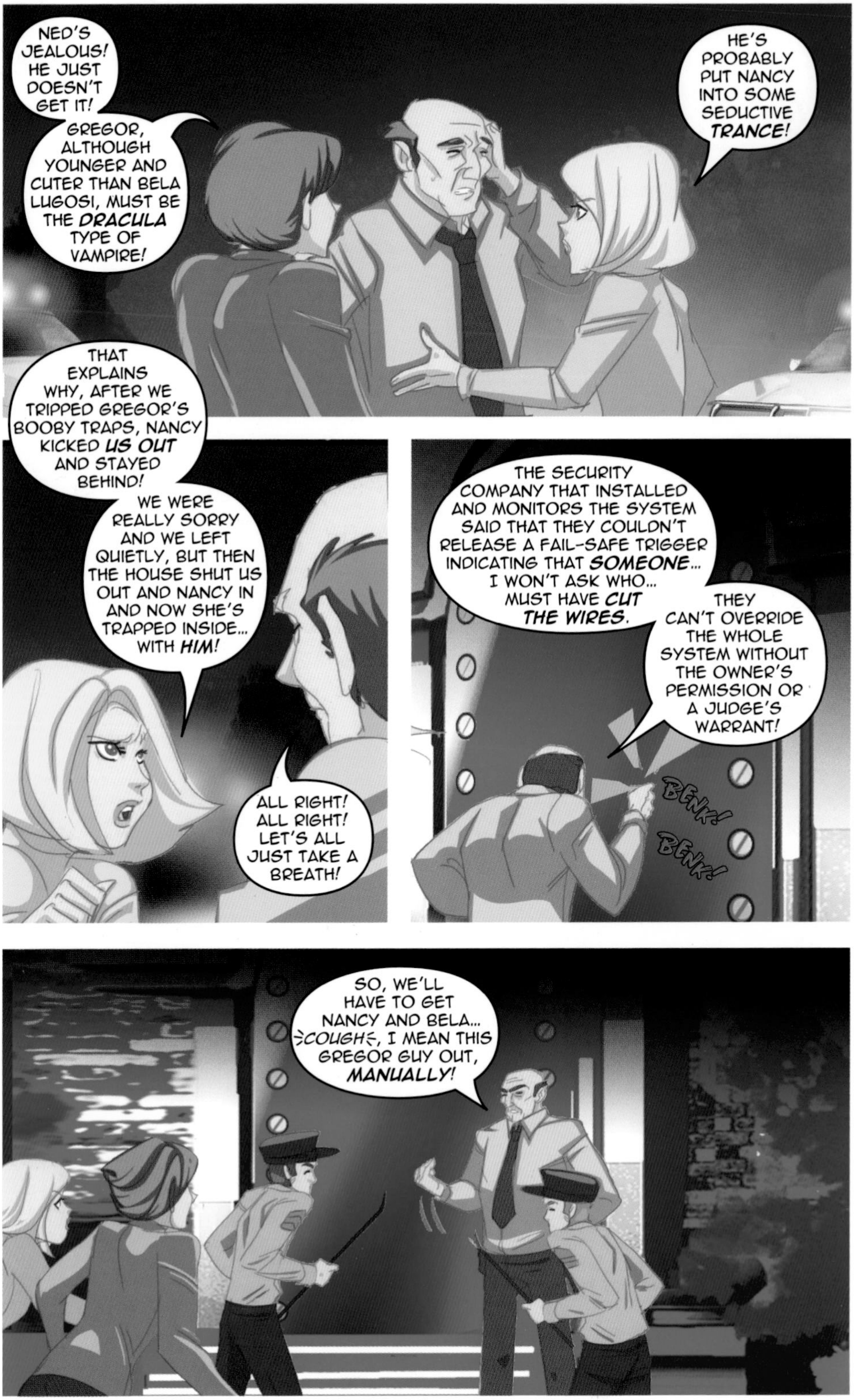
NED'S JEALOUS! HE JUST DOESN'T GET IT!
GREGOR, ALTHOUGH YOUNGER AND CUTER THAN BELA LUGOSI, MUST BE THE DRACULA TYPE OF VAMPIRE!
HE'S PROBABLY PUT NANCY INTO SOME SEDUCTIVE TRANCE!
THAT EXPLAINS WHY, AFTER WE TRIPPED GREGOR'S BOOBY TRAPS, NANCY KICKED US OUT AND STAYED BEHIND!
WE WERE REALLY SORRY AND WE LEFT QUIETLY, BUT THEN THE HOUSE SHUT US OUT AND NANCY IN AND NOW SHE'S TRAPPED INSIDE... WITH HIM!
ALL RIGHT! ALL RIGHT! LET'S ALL JUST TAKE A BREATH!
THE SECURITY COMPANY THAT INSTALLED AND MONITORS THE SYSTEM SAID THAT THEY COULDN'T RELEASE A FAIL-SAFE TRIGGER INDICATING THAT SOMEONE... I WON'T ASK WHO... MUST HAVE CUT THE WIRES.
THEY CAN'T OVERRIDE THE WHOLE SYSTEM WITHOUT THE OWNER'S PERMISSION OR A JUDGE'S WARRANT!
BENK!
BENK!
SO, WE'LL HAVE TO GET NANCY AND BELA... COUGH, I MEAN THIS GREGOR GUY OUT, MANUALLY!

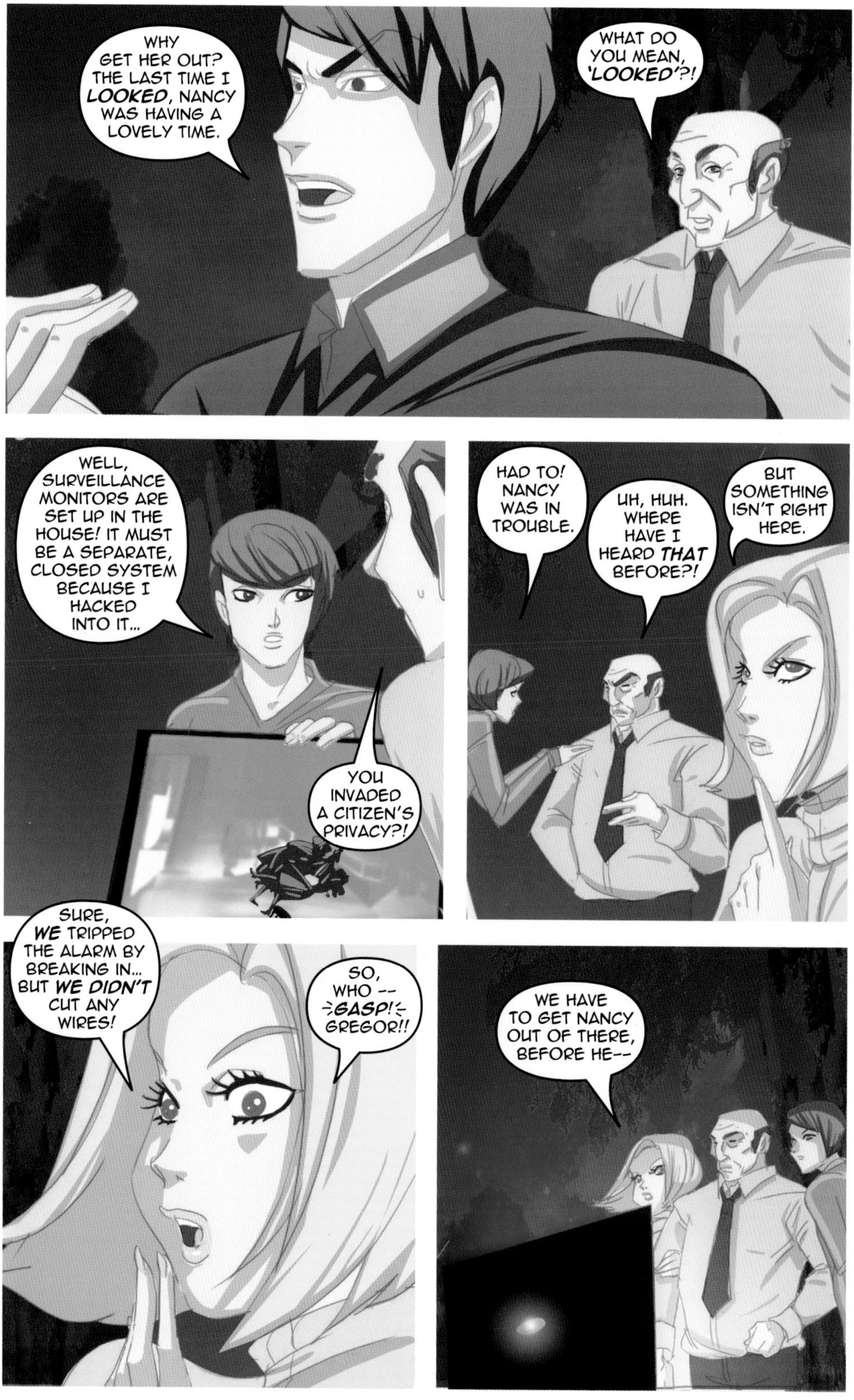
WHY GET HER OUT? THE LAST TIME I LOOKED, NANCY WAS HAVING A LOVELY TIME.
WHAT DO YOU MEAN, 'LOOKED'?!
WELL, SURVEILLANCE MONITORS ARE SET UP IN THE HOUSE! IT MUST BE A SEPARATE, CLOSED SYSTEM BECAUSE I HACKED INTO IT...
YOU INVADED A CITIZEN'S PRIVACY?!
HAD TO! NANCY WAS IN TROUBLE.
UH, HUH. WHERE HAVE I HEARD THAT BEFORE?!
BUT SOMETHING ISN'T RIGHT HERE.
SURE, WE TRIPPED THE ALARM BY BREAKING IN... BUT WE DIDN'T CUT ANY WIRES!
SO, WHO -- GASP! GREGOR!!
WE HAVE TO GET NANCY OUT OF THERE, BEFORE HE--

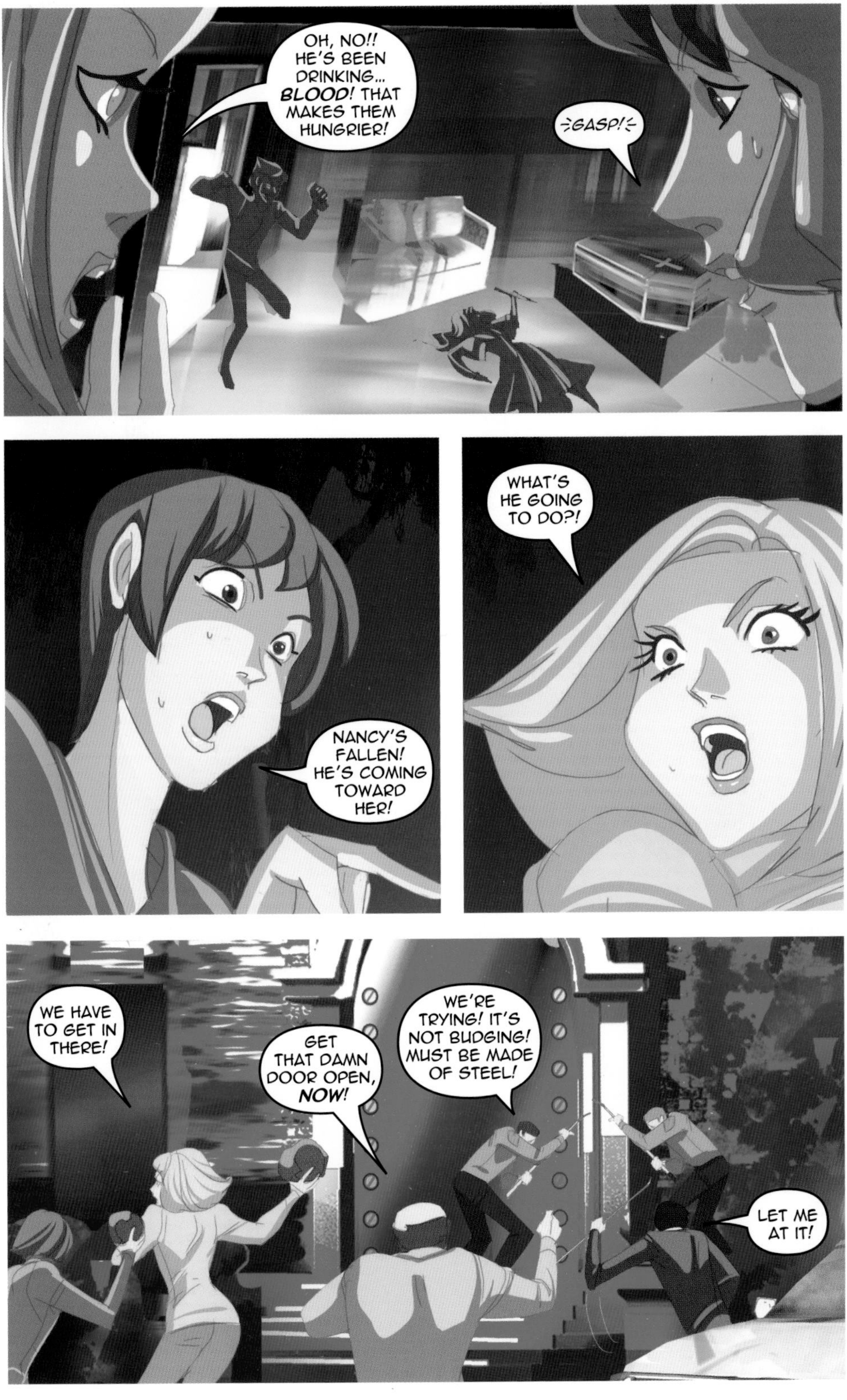
OH, NO!! HE'S BEEN DRINKING... BLOOD! THAT MAKES THEM HUNGRIER!
GASP!
NANCY'S FALLEN! HE'S COMING TOWARD HER!
WHAT'S HE GOING TO DO?!
WE HAVE TO GET IN THERE!
GET THAT DAMN DOOR OPEN, NOW!
WE'RE TRYING! IT'S NOT BUDGING! MUST BE MADE OF STEEL!
LET ME AT IT!

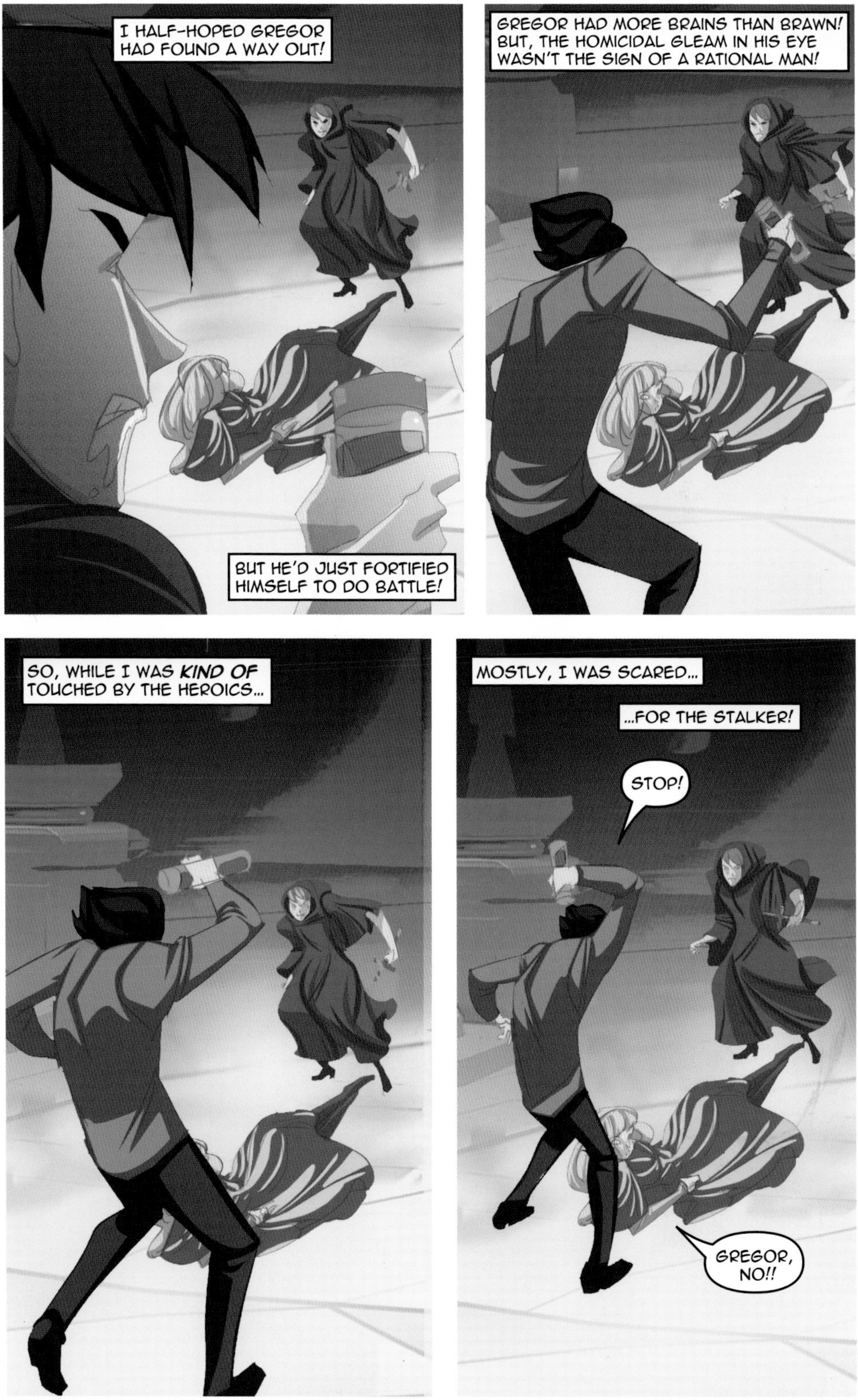
I HALF-HOPED GREGOR HAD FOUND A WAY OUT!
BUT HE'D JUST FORTIFIED HIMSELF TO DO BATTLE!
GREGOR HAD MORE BRAINS THAN BRAWN! BUT, THE HOMICIDAL GLEAM IN HIS EYE WASN'T THE SIGN OF A RATIONAL MAN!
SO, WHILE I WAS KIND OF TOUCHED BY THE HEROICS...
MOSTLY, I WAS SCARED...
...FOR THE STALKER!
STOP!
GREGOR, NO!!

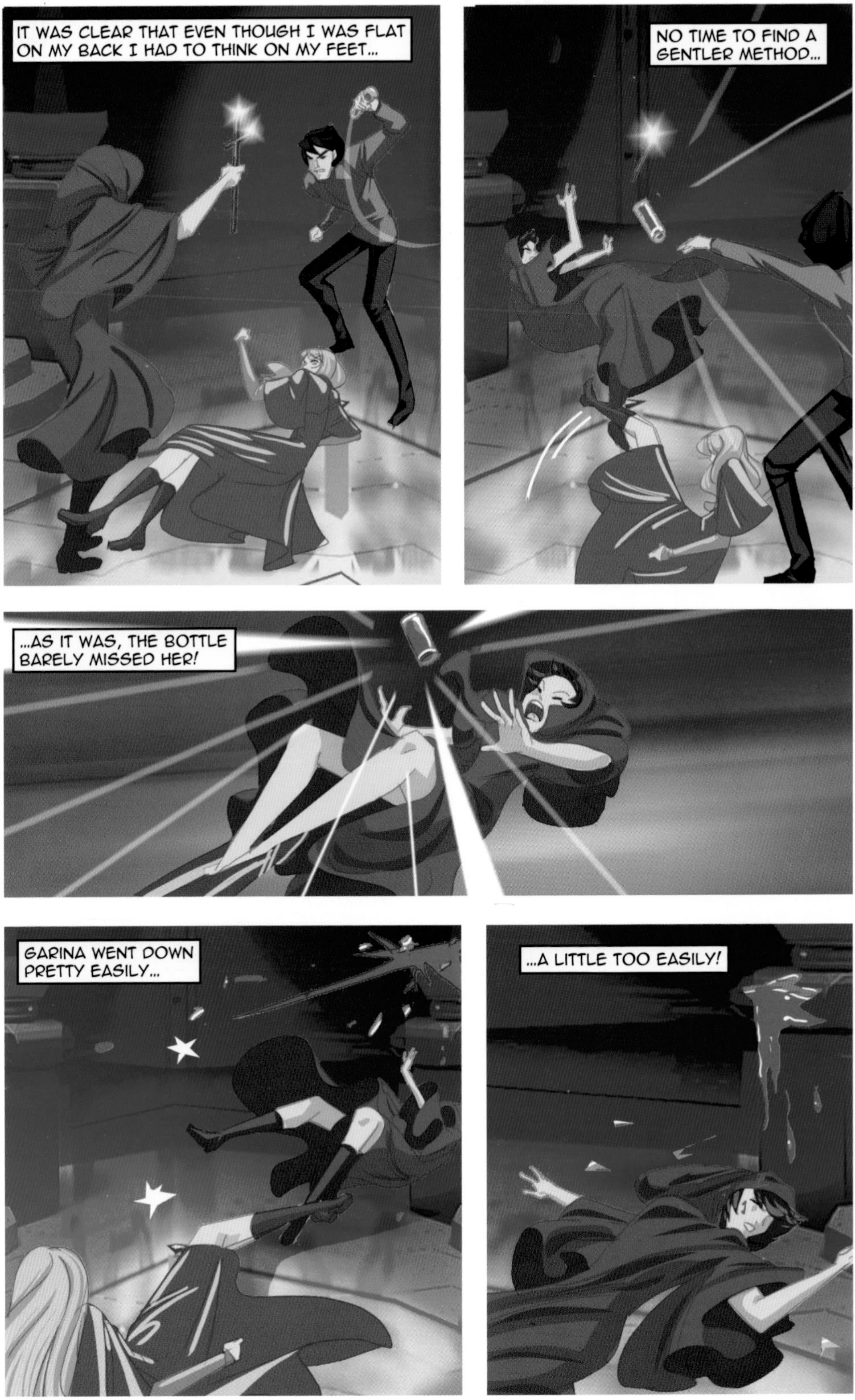
IT WAS CLEAR THAT EVEN THOUGH I WAS FLAT ON MY BACK I HAD TO THINK ON MY FEET...
NO TIME TO FIND A GENTLER METHOD...
...AS IT WAS, THE BOTTLE BARELY MISSED HER!
GARINA WENT DOWN PRETTY EASILY...
...A LITTLE TOO EASILY!

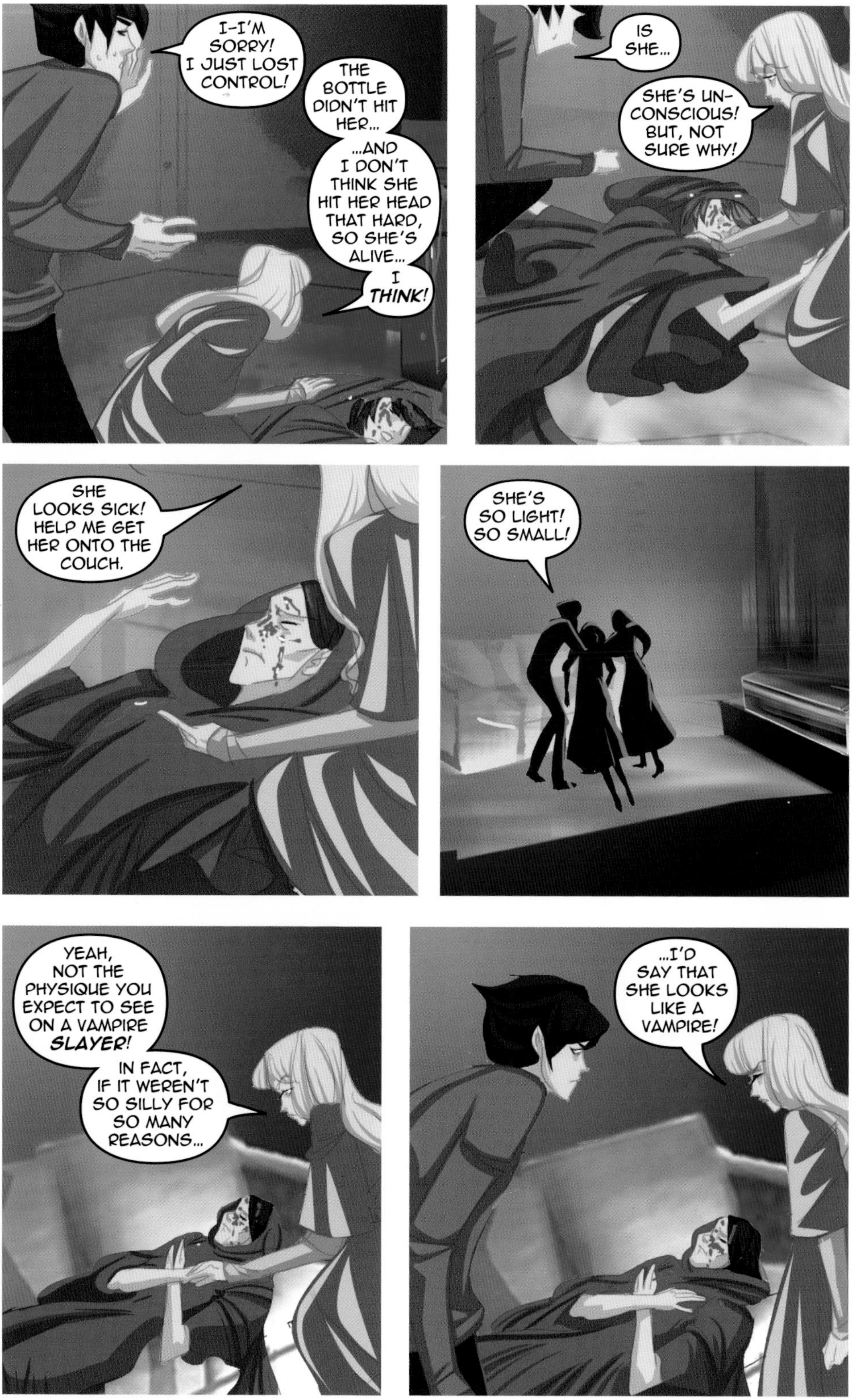
I-I'M SORRY! I JUST LOST CONTROL!
THE BOTTLE DIDN'T HIT HER...
...AND I DON'T THINK SHE HIT HER HEAD THAT HARD, SO SHE'S ALIVE...
I *THINK*!
IS SHE...
SHE'S UN-CONSCIOUS! BUT, NOT SURE WHY!
SHE LOOKS SICK! HELP ME GET HER ONTO THE COUCH.
SHE'S SO LIGHT! SO SMALL!
YEAH, NOT THE PHYSIQUE YOU EXPECT TO SEE ON A VAMPIRE *SLAYER*!
IN FACT, IF IT WEREN'T SO SILLY FOR SO MANY REASONS...
...I'D SAY THAT SHE LOOKS LIKE A VAMPIRE!

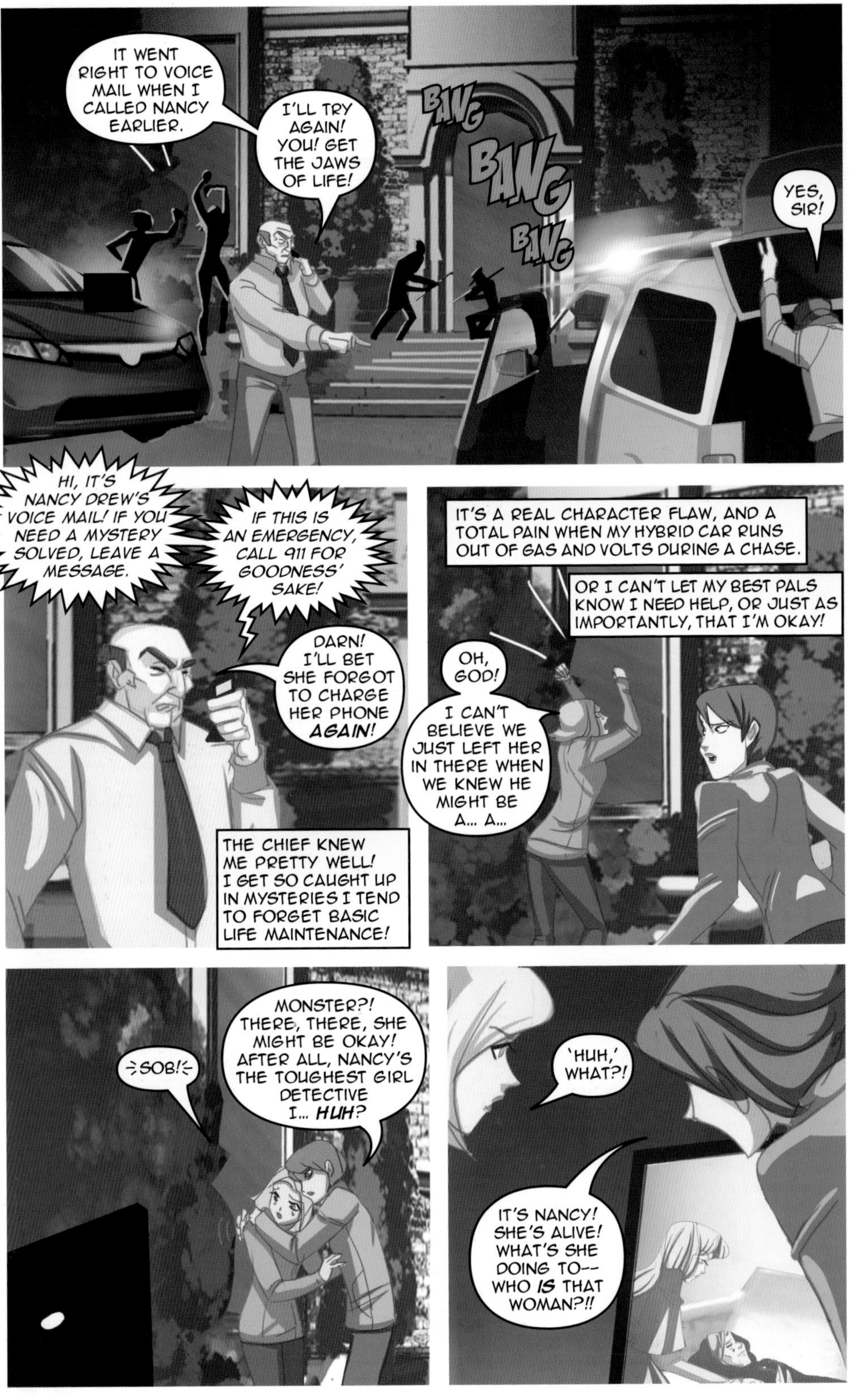
IT WENT RIGHT TO VOICE MAIL WHEN I CALLED NANCY EARLIER.
I'LL TRY AGAIN! YOU! GET THE JAWS OF LIFE!
BANG
BANG
BANG
YES, SIR!
HI, IT'S NANCY DREW'S VOICE MAIL! IF YOU NEED A MYSTERY SOLVED, LEAVE A MESSAGE.
IF THIS IS AN EMERGENCY, CALL 911 FOR GOODNESS' SAKE!
DARN! I'LL BET SHE FORGOT TO CHARGE HER PHONE AGAIN!
THE CHIEF KNEW ME PRETTY WELL! I GET SO CAUGHT UP IN MYSTERIES I TEND TO FORGET BASIC LIFE MAINTENANCE!
IT'S A REAL CHARACTER FLAW, AND A TOTAL PAIN WHEN MY HYBRID CAR RUNS OUT OF GAS AND VOLTS DURING A CHASE.
OR I CAN'T LET MY BEST PALS KNOW I NEED HELP, OR JUST AS IMPORTANTLY, THAT I'M OKAY!
OH, GOD!
I CAN'T BELIEVE WE JUST LEFT HER IN THERE WHEN WE KNEW HE MIGHT BE A... A...
SOB!
MONSTER?! THERE, THERE, SHE MIGHT BE OKAY! AFTER ALL, NANCY'S THE TOUGHEST GIRL DETECTIVE I... HUH?
'HUH,' WHAT?!
IT'S NANCY! SHE'S ALIVE! WHAT'S SHE DOING TO-- WHO IS THAT WOMAN?!!

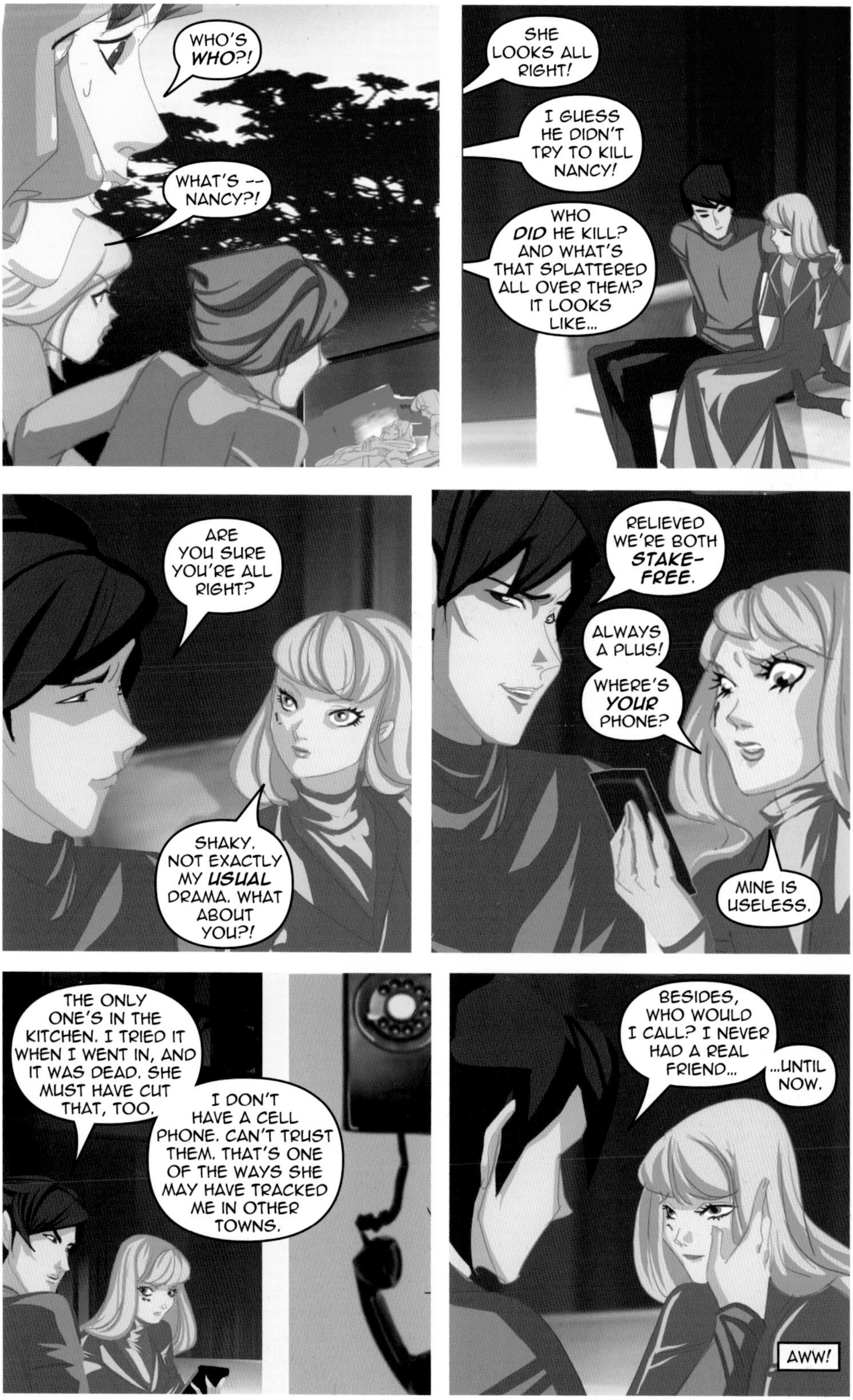
WHO'S *WHO*?!
WHAT'S -- NANCY?!
SHE LOOKS ALL RIGHT!
I GUESS HE DIDN'T TRY TO KILL NANCY!
WHO *DID* HE KILL? AND WHAT'S THAT SPLATTERED ALL OVER THEM? IT LOOKS LIKE...
ARE YOU SURE YOU'RE ALL RIGHT?
SHAKY. NOT EXACTLY MY *USUAL* DRAMA. WHAT ABOUT YOU?!
RELIEVED WE'RE BOTH *STAKE-FREE*.
ALWAYS A PLUS!
WHERE'S *YOUR* PHONE?
MINE IS USELESS.
THE ONLY ONE'S IN THE KITCHEN. I TRIED IT WHEN I WENT IN, AND IT WAS DEAD. SHE MUST HAVE CUT THAT, TOO.
I DON'T HAVE A CELL PHONE. CAN'T TRUST THEM. THAT'S ONE OF THE WAYS SHE MAY HAVE TRACKED ME IN OTHER TOWNS.
BESIDES, WHO WOULD I CALL? I NEVER HAD A REAL FRIEND...
...UNTIL NOW.
AWW!

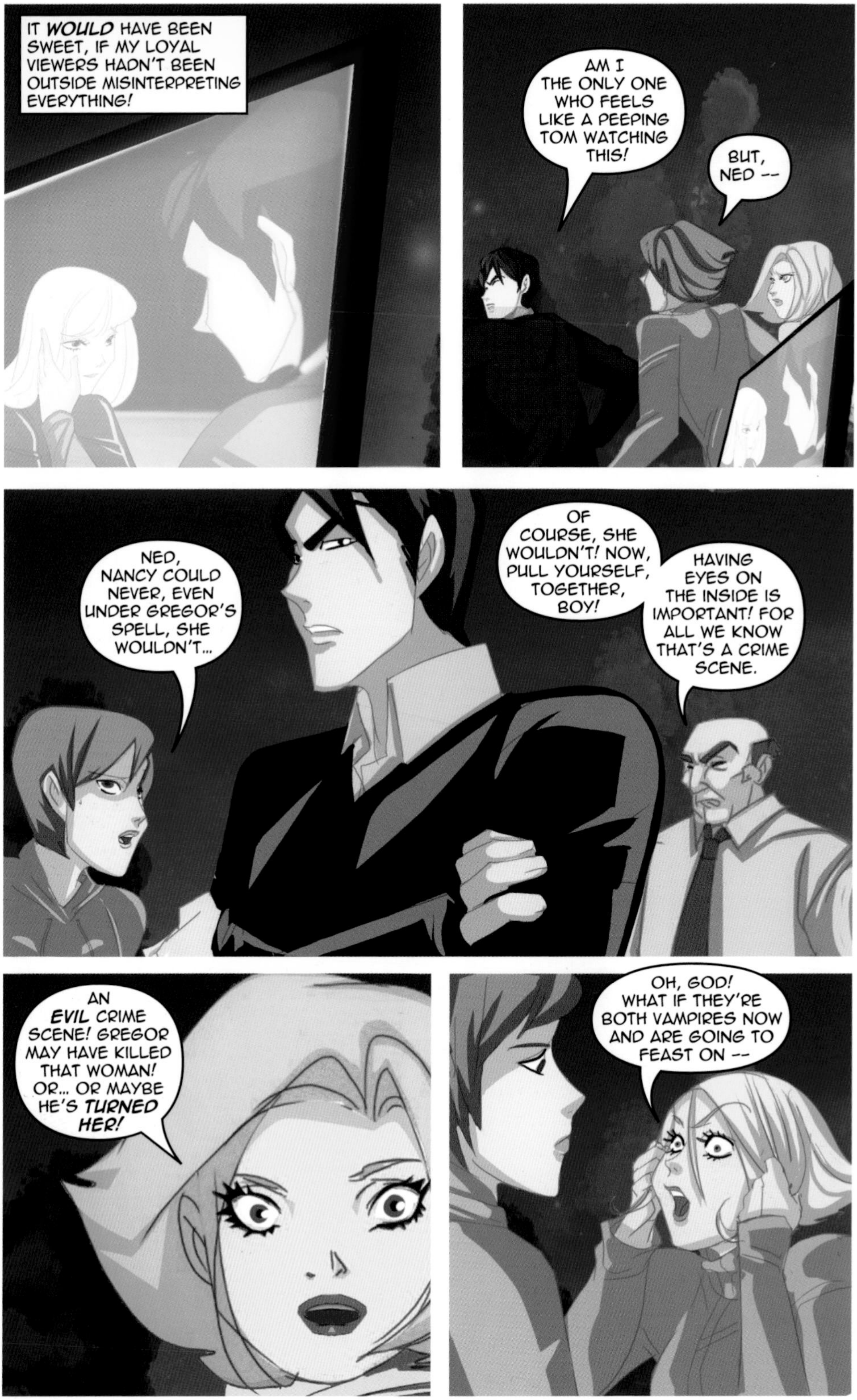
IT ***WOULD*** HAVE BEEN SWEET, IF MY LOYAL VIEWERS HADN'T BEEN OUTSIDE MISINTERPRETING EVERYTHING!
AM I THE ONLY ONE WHO FEELS LIKE A PEEPING TOM WATCHING THIS!
BUT, NED --
NED, NANCY COULD NEVER, EVEN UNDER GREGOR'S SPELL, SHE WOULDN'T...
OF COURSE, SHE WOULDN'T! NOW, PULL YOURSELF TOGETHER, BOY!
HAVING EYES ON THE INSIDE IS IMPORTANT! FOR ALL WE KNOW THAT'S A CRIME SCENE.
AN ***EVIL*** CRIME SCENE! GREGOR MAY HAVE KILLED THAT WOMAN! OR... OR MAYBE HE'S ***TURNED HER!***
OH, GOD! WHAT IF THEY'RE BOTH VAMPIRES NOW AND ARE GOING TO FEAST ON --

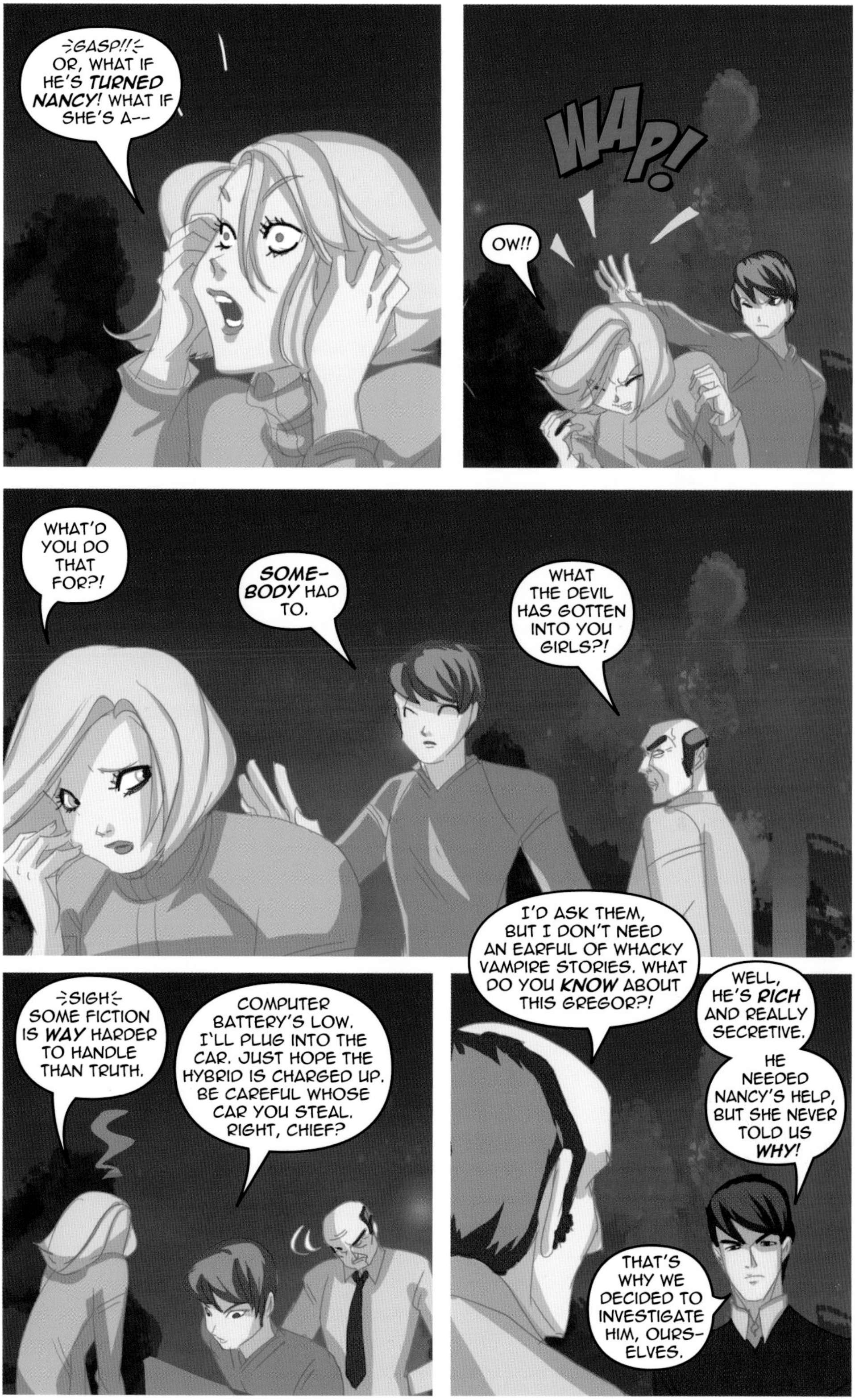
⊰GASP!!⊱ OR, WHAT IF HE'S TURNED NANCY! WHAT IF SHE'S A--
WAP!
OW!!
WHAT'D YOU DO THAT FOR?!
SOME-BODY HAD TO.
WHAT THE DEVIL HAS GOTTEN INTO YOU GIRLS?!
⊰SIGH⊱ SOME FICTION IS WAY HARDER TO HANDLE THAN TRUTH.
COMPUTER BATTERY'S LOW. I'LL PLUG INTO THE CAR. JUST HOPE THE HYBRID IS CHARGED UP. BE CAREFUL WHOSE CAR YOU STEAL. RIGHT, CHIEF?
I'D ASK THEM, BUT I DON'T NEED AN EARFUL OF WHACKY VAMPIRE STORIES. WHAT DO YOU KNOW ABOUT THIS GREGOR?!
WELL, HE'S RICH AND REALLY SECRETIVE.
HE NEEDED NANCY'S HELP, BUT SHE NEVER TOLD US WHY!
THAT'S WHY WE DECIDED TO INVESTIGATE HIM, OURS-ELVES.

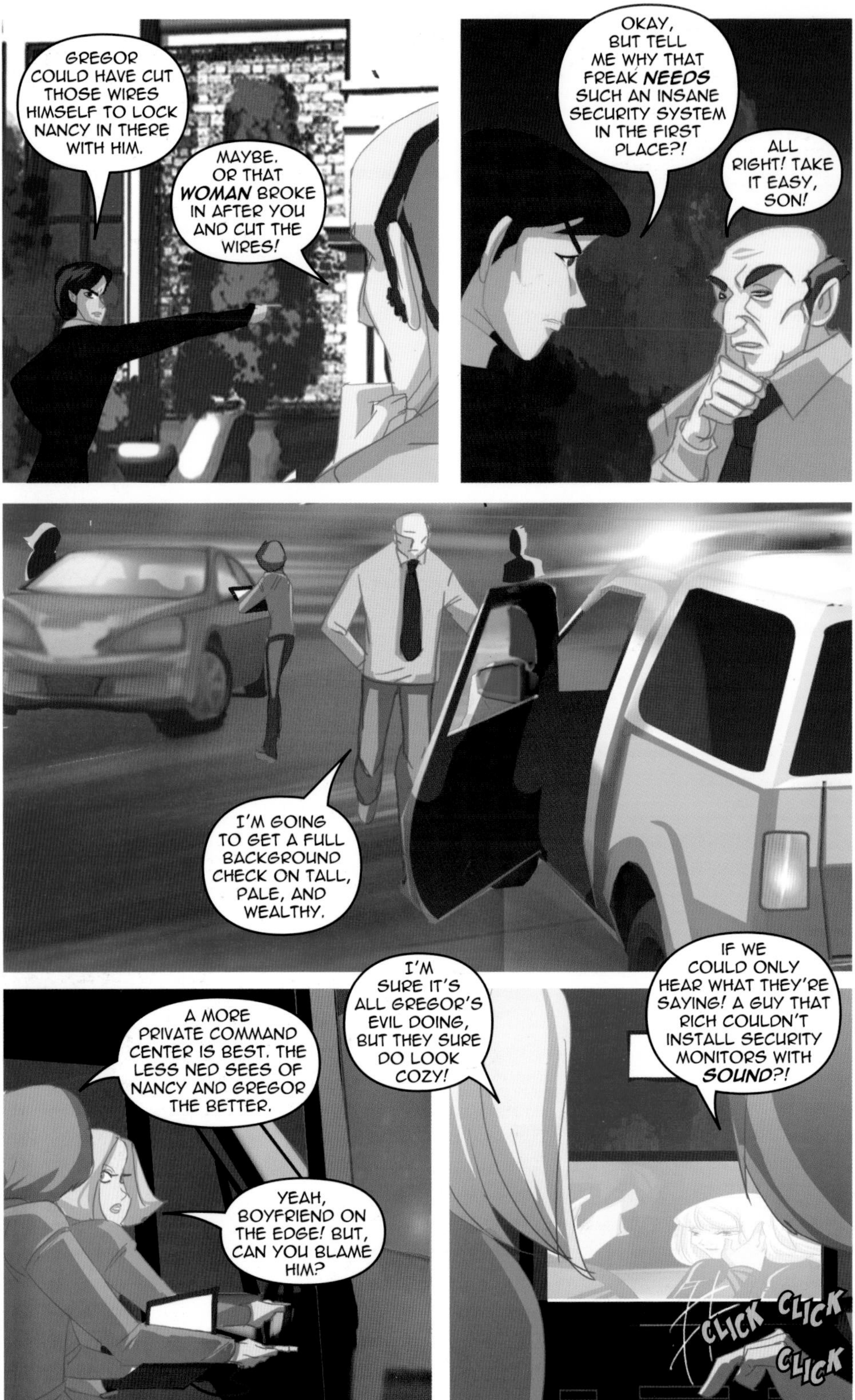
GREGOR COULD HAVE CUT THOSE WIRES HIMSELF TO LOCK NANCY IN THERE WITH HIM.
MAYBE. OR THAT **WOMAN** BROKE IN AFTER YOU AND CUT THE WIRES!
OKAY, BUT TELL ME WHY THAT FREAK **NEEDS** SUCH AN INSANE SECURITY SYSTEM IN THE FIRST PLACE?!
ALL RIGHT! TAKE IT EASY, SON!
I'M GOING TO GET A FULL BACKGROUND CHECK ON TALL, PALE, AND WEALTHY.
A MORE PRIVATE COMMAND CENTER IS BEST. THE LESS NED SEES OF NANCY AND GREGOR THE BETTER.
YEAH, BOYFRIEND ON THE EDGE! BUT, CAN YOU BLAME HIM?
I'M SURE IT'S ALL GREGOR'S EVIL DOING, BUT THEY SURE DO LOOK COZY!
IF WE COULD ONLY HEAR WHAT THEY'RE SAYING! A GUY THAT RICH COULDN'T INSTALL SECURITY MONITORS WITH **SOUND**?!
CLICK CLICK
CLICK

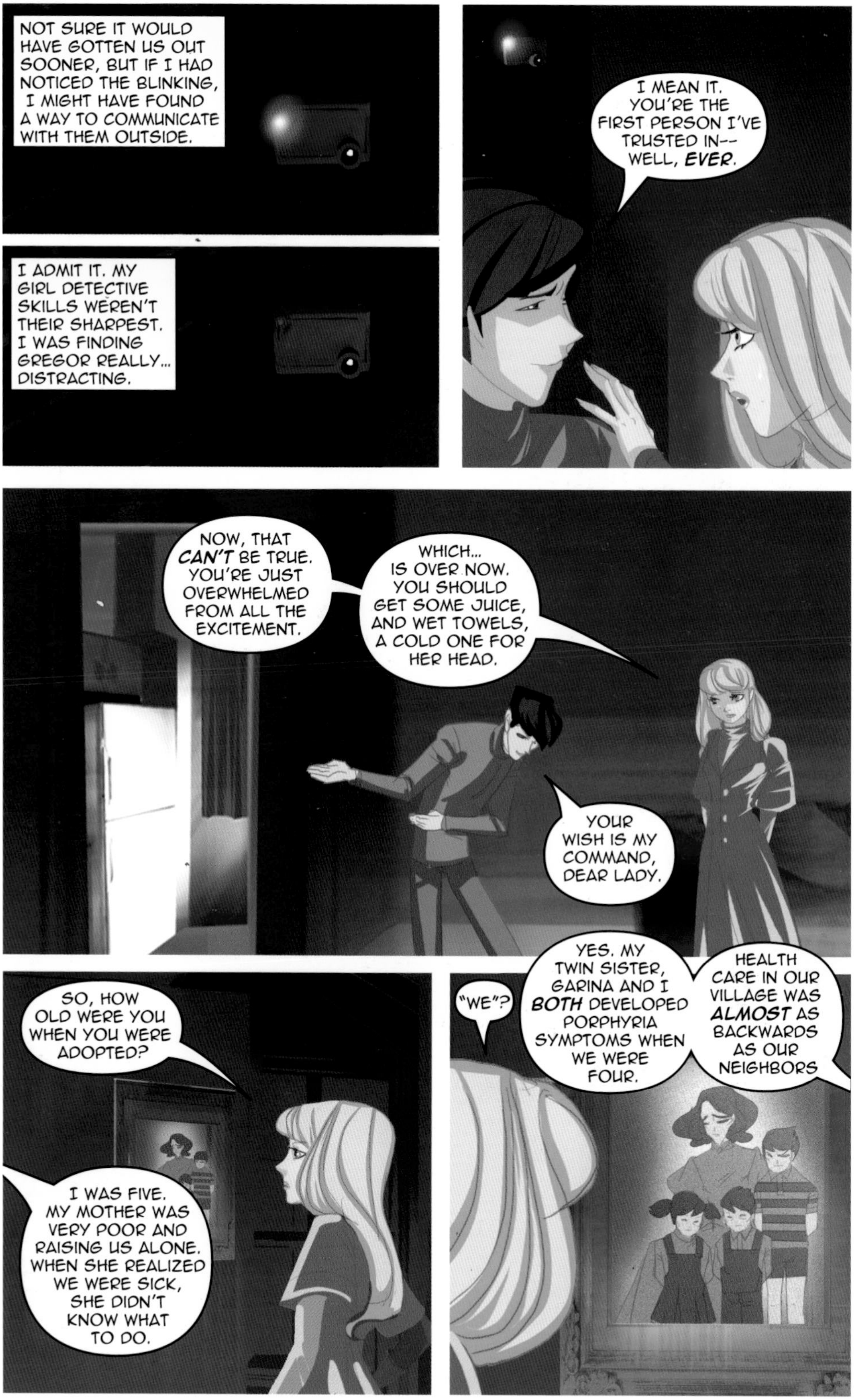
NOT SURE IT WOULD HAVE GOTTEN US OUT SOONER, BUT IF I HAD NOTICED THE BLINKING, I MIGHT HAVE FOUND A WAY TO COMMUNICATE WITH THEM OUTSIDE.
I ADMIT IT. MY GIRL DETECTIVE SKILLS WEREN'T THEIR SHARPEST. I WAS FINDING GREGOR REALLY... DISTRACTING.
I MEAN IT. YOU'RE THE FIRST PERSON I'VE TRUSTED IN-- WELL, *EVER*.
NOW, THAT *CAN'T* BE TRUE. YOU'RE JUST OVERWHELMED FROM ALL THE EXCITEMENT.
WHICH... IS OVER NOW. YOU SHOULD GET SOME JUICE, AND WET TOWELS, A COLD ONE FOR HER HEAD.
YOUR WISH IS MY COMMAND, DEAR LADY.
SO, HOW OLD WERE YOU WHEN YOU WERE ADOPTED?
I WAS FIVE. MY MOTHER WAS VERY POOR AND RAISING US ALONE. WHEN SHE REALIZED WE WERE SICK, SHE DIDN'T KNOW WHAT TO DO.
"WE"?
YES. MY TWIN SISTER, GARINA AND I *BOTH* DEVELOPED PORPHYRIA SYMPTOMS WHEN WE WERE FOUR.
HEALTH CARE IN OUR VILLAGE WAS *ALMOST* AS BACKWARDS AS OUR NEIGHBORS

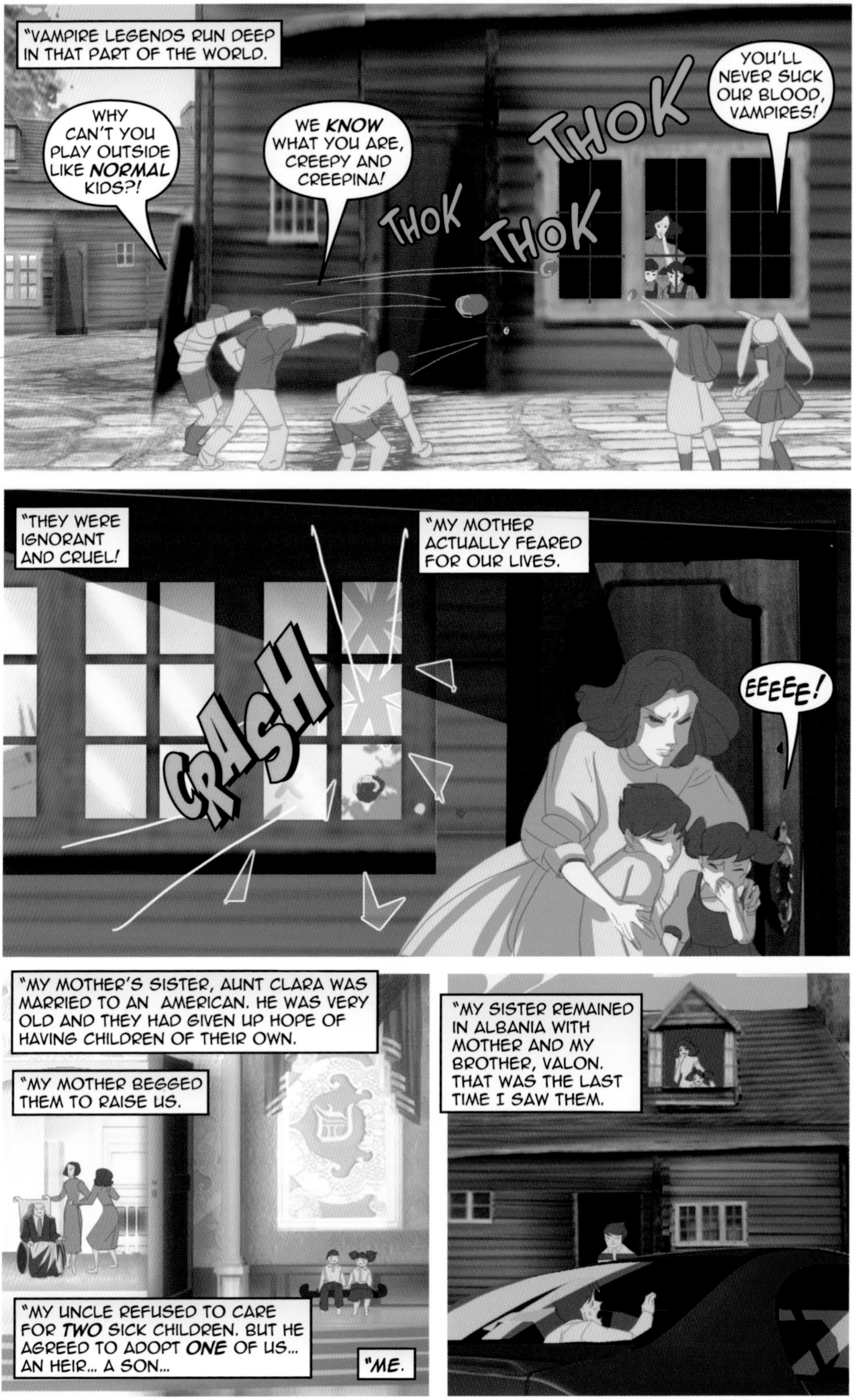
"VAMPIRE LEGENDS RUN DEEP IN THAT PART OF THE WORLD.
WHY CAN'T YOU PLAY OUTSIDE LIKE NORMAL KIDS?!
WE KNOW WHAT YOU ARE, CREEPY AND CREEPINA!
THOK
THOK
THOK
YOU'LL NEVER SUCK OUR BLOOD, VAMPIRES!
"THEY WERE IGNORANT AND CRUEL!
CRASH
"MY MOTHER ACTUALLY FEARED FOR OUR LIVES.
EEEEE!
"MY MOTHER'S SISTER, AUNT CLARA WAS MARRIED TO AN AMERICAN. HE WAS VERY OLD AND THEY HAD GIVEN UP HOPE OF HAVING CHILDREN OF THEIR OWN.
"MY MOTHER BEGGED THEM TO RAISE US.
"MY UNCLE REFUSED TO CARE FOR TWO SICK CHILDREN. BUT HE AGREED TO ADOPT ONE OF US... AN HEIR... A SON...
"ME.
"MY SISTER REMAINED IN ALBANIA WITH MOTHER AND MY BROTHER, VALON. THAT WAS THE LAST TIME I SAW THEM.

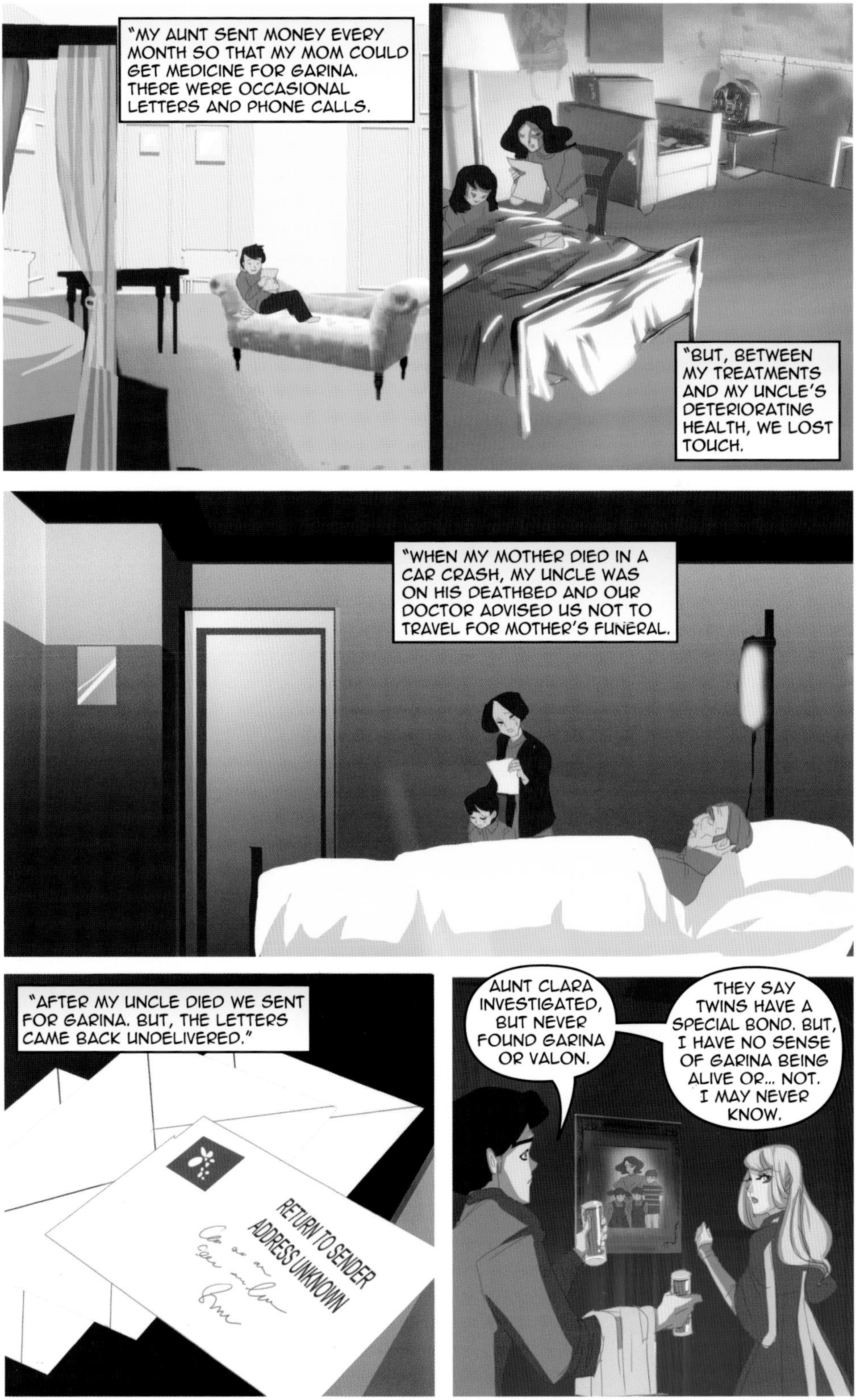
"MY AUNT SENT MONEY EVERY MONTH SO THAT MY MOM COULD GET MEDICINE FOR GARINA. THERE WERE OCCASIONAL LETTERS AND PHONE CALLS.
"BUT, BETWEEN MY TREATMENTS AND MY UNCLE'S DETERIORATING HEALTH, WE LOST TOUCH.
"WHEN MY MOTHER DIED IN A CAR CRASH, MY UNCLE WAS ON HIS DEATHBED AND OUR DOCTOR ADVISED US NOT TO TRAVEL FOR MOTHER'S FUNERAL.
"AFTER MY UNCLE DIED WE SENT FOR GARINA. BUT, THE LETTERS CAME BACK UNDELIVERED."
RETURN TO SENDER
ADDRESS UNKNOWN
AUNT CLARA INVESTIGATED, BUT NEVER FOUND GARINA OR VALON.
THEY SAY TWINS HAVE A SPECIAL BOND. BUT, I HAVE NO SENSE OF GARINA BEING ALIVE OR... NOT. I MAY NEVER KNOW.

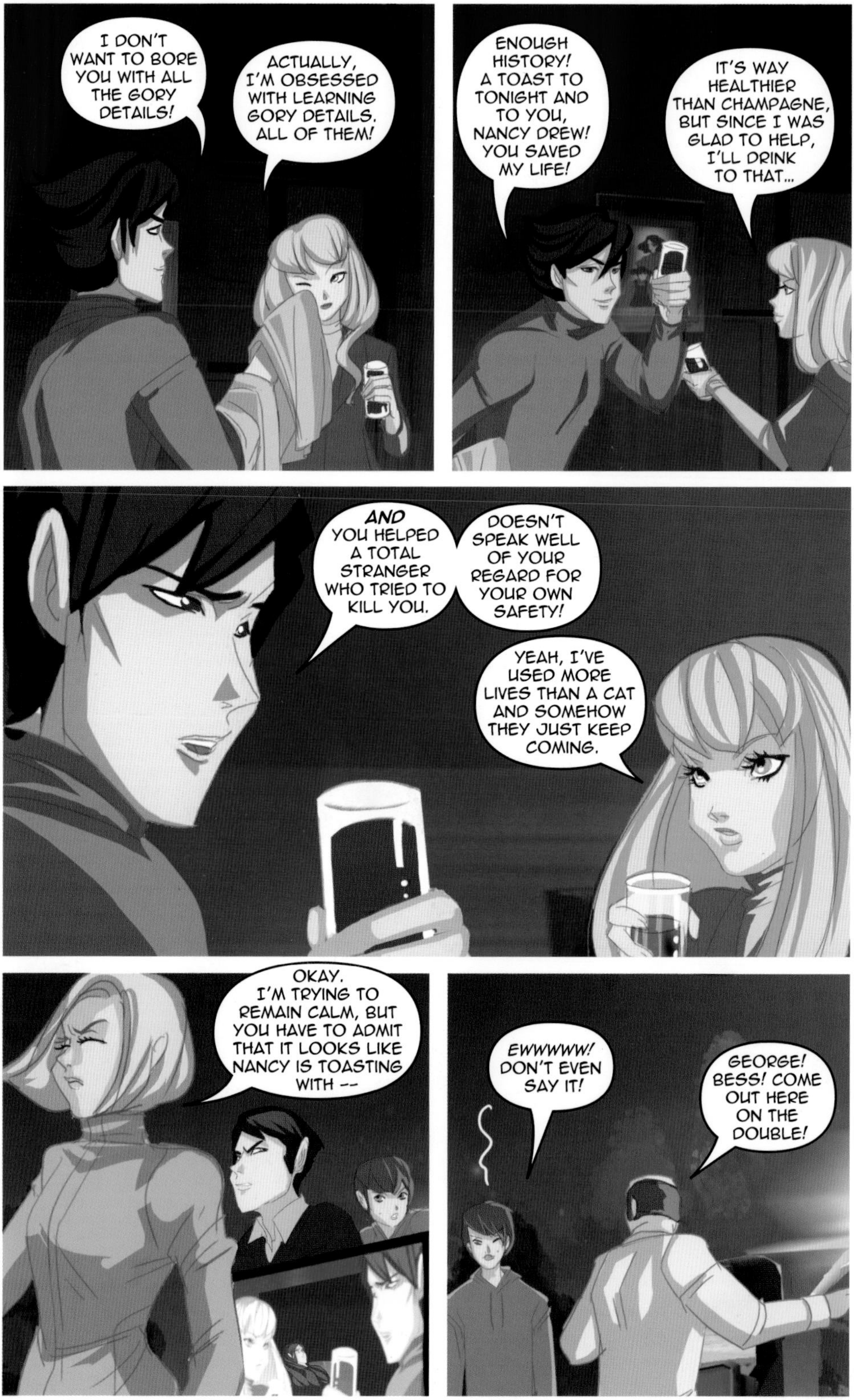
I DON'T WANT TO BORE YOU WITH ALL THE GORY DETAILS!
ACTUALLY, I'M OBSESSED WITH LEARNING GORY DETAILS. ALL OF THEM!
ENOUGH HISTORY! A TOAST TO TONIGHT AND TO YOU, NANCY DREW! YOU SAVED MY LIFE!
IT'S WAY HEALTHIER THAN CHAMPAGNE, BUT SINCE I WAS GLAD TO HELP, I'LL DRINK TO THAT...
AND YOU HELPED A TOTAL STRANGER WHO TRIED TO KILL YOU.
DOESN'T SPEAK WELL OF YOUR REGARD FOR YOUR OWN SAFETY!
YEAH, I'VE USED MORE LIVES THAN A CAT AND SOMEHOW THEY JUST KEEP COMING.
OKAY. I'M TRYING TO REMAIN CALM, BUT YOU HAVE TO ADMIT THAT IT LOOKS LIKE NANCY IS TOASTING WITH --
EWWWWW! DON'T EVEN SAY IT!
GEORGE! BESS! COME OUT HERE ON THE DOUBLE!

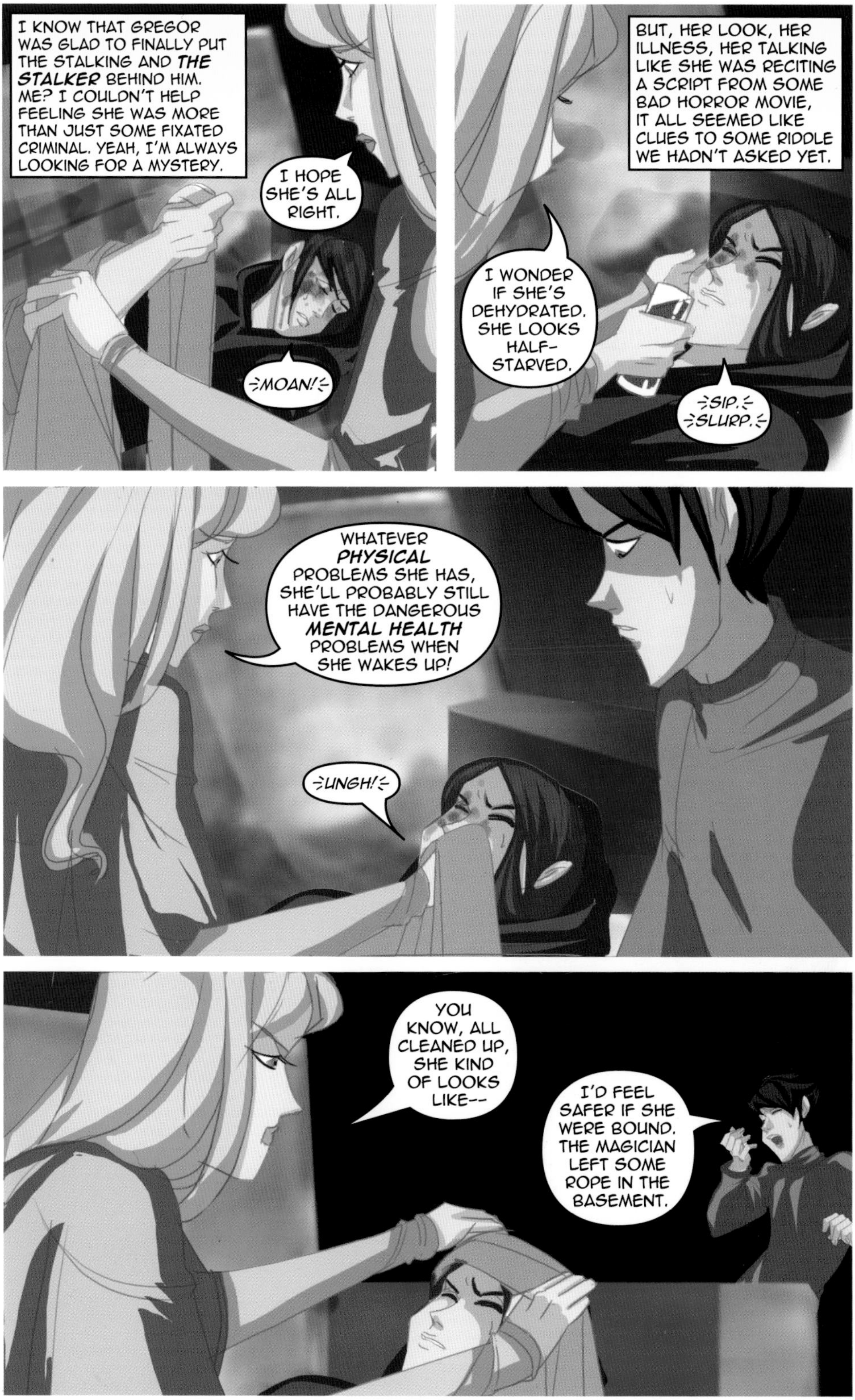

I KNOW THAT GREGOR WAS GLAD TO FINALLY PUT THE STALKING AND *THE STALKER* BEHIND HIM. ME? I COULDN'T HELP FEELING SHE WAS MORE THAN JUST SOME FIXATED CRIMINAL. YEAH, I'M ALWAYS LOOKING FOR A MYSTERY.
I HOPE SHE'S ALL RIGHT.
MOAN!
BUT, HER LOOK, HER ILLNESS, HER TALKING LIKE SHE WAS RECITING A SCRIPT FROM SOME BAD HORROR MOVIE, IT ALL SEEMED LIKE CLUES TO SOME RIDDLE WE HADN'T ASKED YET.
I WONDER IF SHE'S DEHYDRATED. SHE LOOKS HALF-STARVED.
SIP. SLURP.
WHATEVER *PHYSICAL* PROBLEMS SHE HAS, SHE'LL PROBABLY STILL HAVE THE DANGEROUS *MENTAL HEALTH* PROBLEMS WHEN SHE WAKES UP!
UNGH!
YOU KNOW, ALL CLEANED UP, SHE KIND OF LOOKS LIKE--
I'D FEEL SAFER IF SHE WERE BOUND. THE MAGICIAN LEFT SOME ROPE IN THE BASEMENT.

WAKING UP WITH ROPE AROUND MY WRISTS ALWAYS MAKES ME **MORE** AGITATED! NOT LESS. I MADE THE MISTAKE OF TRYING TO LIGHTEN THINGS UP.

YOU WOULDN'T HAPPEN TO HAVE A NICE, COMFY STRAIGHT JACKET?

WHY WOULD YOU SAY **THAT**?! WHAT DO YOU **MEAN**?!

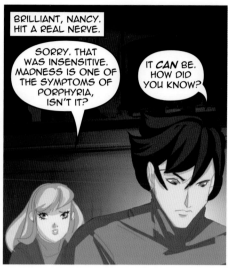

BRILLIANT, NANCY. HIT A REAL NERVE.

SORRY. THAT WAS INSENSITIVE. MADNESS IS ONE OF THE SYMPTOMS OF PORPHYRIA, ISN'T IT?

IT **CAN** BE. HOW DID YOU KNOW?

MY MIND'S PACKED WITH INFO THAT ISN'T **ALWAYS** USELESS. THEY NOW THINK KING GEORGE III PROBABLY HAD PORPHYRIA. BACK BEFORE THEY KNEW WHAT TO CALL IT OR HOW TO TREAT IT.

GUY HAD THE BEST DOCTORS AVAILABLE, BUT STILL WOUND UP IN A STRAIGHT JACKET.

WHEN YOU'RE SICK, IT'S EASY TO FORGET THAT MEDICAL SCIENCE HAS COME A LONG WAY IN 200 YEARS! THE FUTURE CAN START TO LOOK BLEAK.

THEN SOMETHING BRINGS YOU RIGHT BACK TO THE PRESENT.

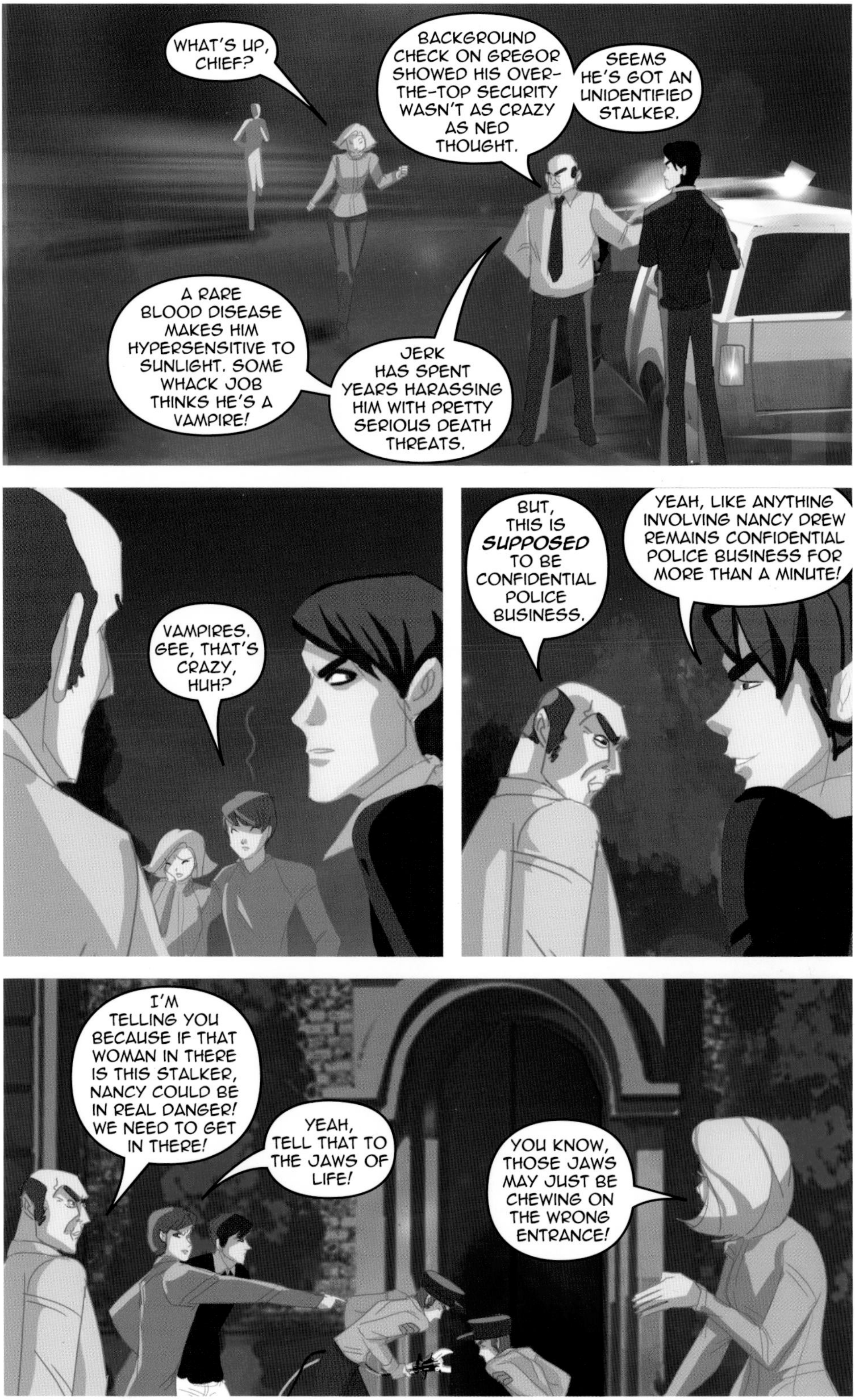
WHAT'S UP, CHIEF?
BACKGROUND CHECK ON GREGOR SHOWED HIS OVER-THE-TOP SECURITY WASN'T AS CRAZY AS NED THOUGHT.
SEEMS HE'S GOT AN UNIDENTIFIED STALKER.
A RARE BLOOD DISEASE MAKES HIM HYPERSENSITIVE TO SUNLIGHT. SOME WHACK JOB THINKS HE'S A VAMPIRE!
JERK HAS SPENT YEARS HARASSING HIM WITH PRETTY SERIOUS DEATH THREATS.
VAMPIRES. GEE, THAT'S CRAZY, HUH?
BUT, THIS IS *SUPPOSED* TO BE CONFIDENTIAL POLICE BUSINESS.
YEAH, LIKE ANYTHING INVOLVING NANCY DREW REMAINS CONFIDENTIAL POLICE BUSINESS FOR MORE THAN A MINUTE!
I'M TELLING YOU BECAUSE IF THAT WOMAN IN THERE IS THIS STALKER, NANCY COULD BE IN REAL DANGER! WE NEED TO GET IN THERE!
YEAH, TELL THAT TO THE JAWS OF LIFE!
YOU KNOW, THOSE JAWS MAY JUST BE CHEWING ON THE WRONG ENTRANCE!

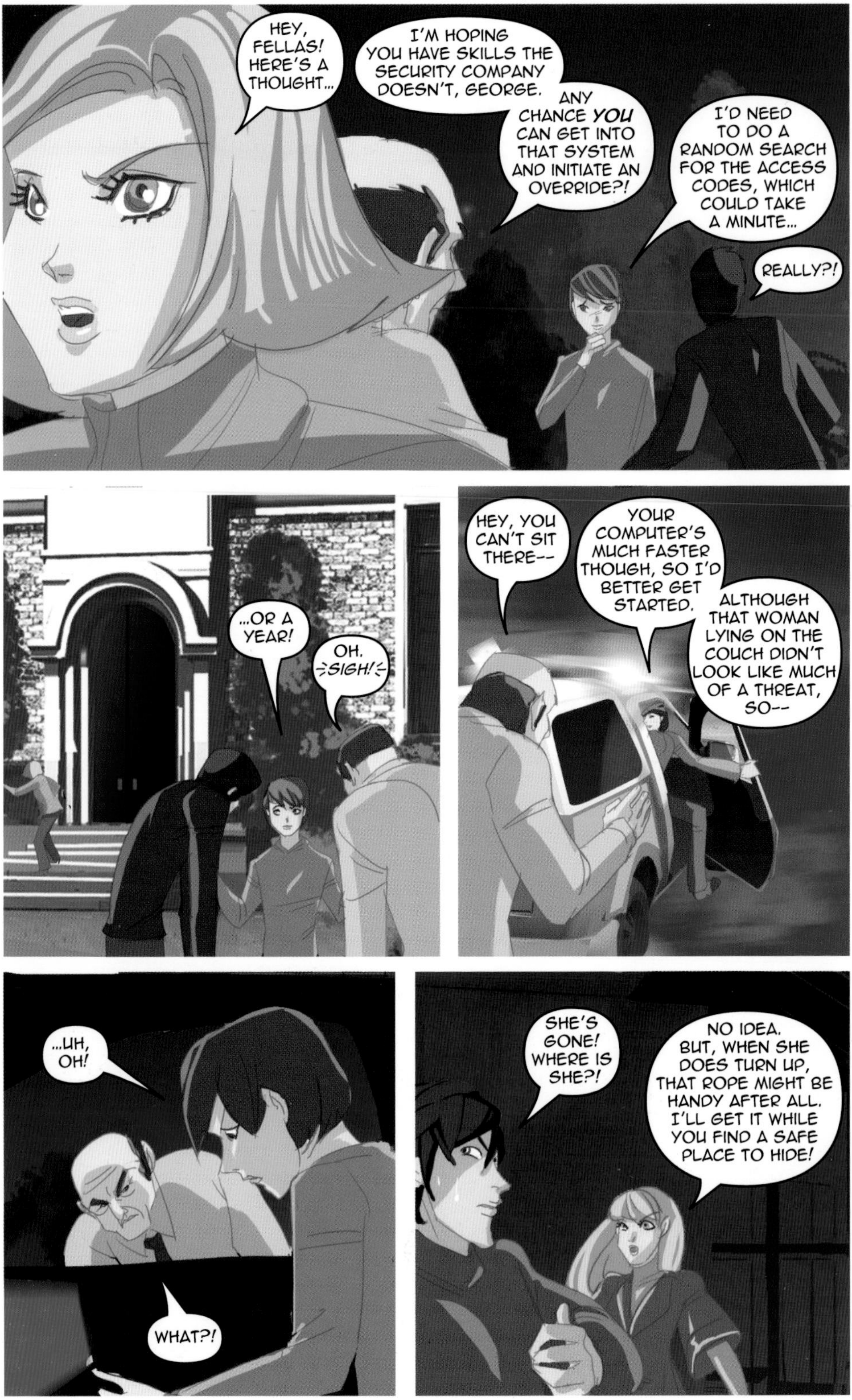

HEY, FELLAS! HERE'S A THOUGHT...
I'M HOPING YOU HAVE SKILLS THE SECURITY COMPANY DOESN'T, GEORGE.
ANY CHANCE *YOU* CAN GET INTO THAT SYSTEM AND INITIATE AN OVERRIDE?!
I'D NEED TO DO A RANDOM SEARCH FOR THE ACCESS CODES, WHICH COULD TAKE A MINUTE...
REALLY?!
...OR A YEAR!
OH. *SIGH!*
HEY, YOU CAN'T SIT THERE--
YOUR COMPUTER'S MUCH FASTER THOUGH, SO I'D BETTER GET STARTED.
ALTHOUGH THAT WOMAN LYING ON THE COUCH DIDN'T LOOK LIKE MUCH OF A THREAT, SO--
...UH, OH!
WHAT?!
SHE'S GONE! WHERE IS SHE?!
NO IDEA. BUT, WHEN SHE DOES TURN UP, THAT ROPE MIGHT BE HANDY AFTER ALL. I'LL GET IT WHILE YOU FIND A SAFE PLACE TO HIDE!

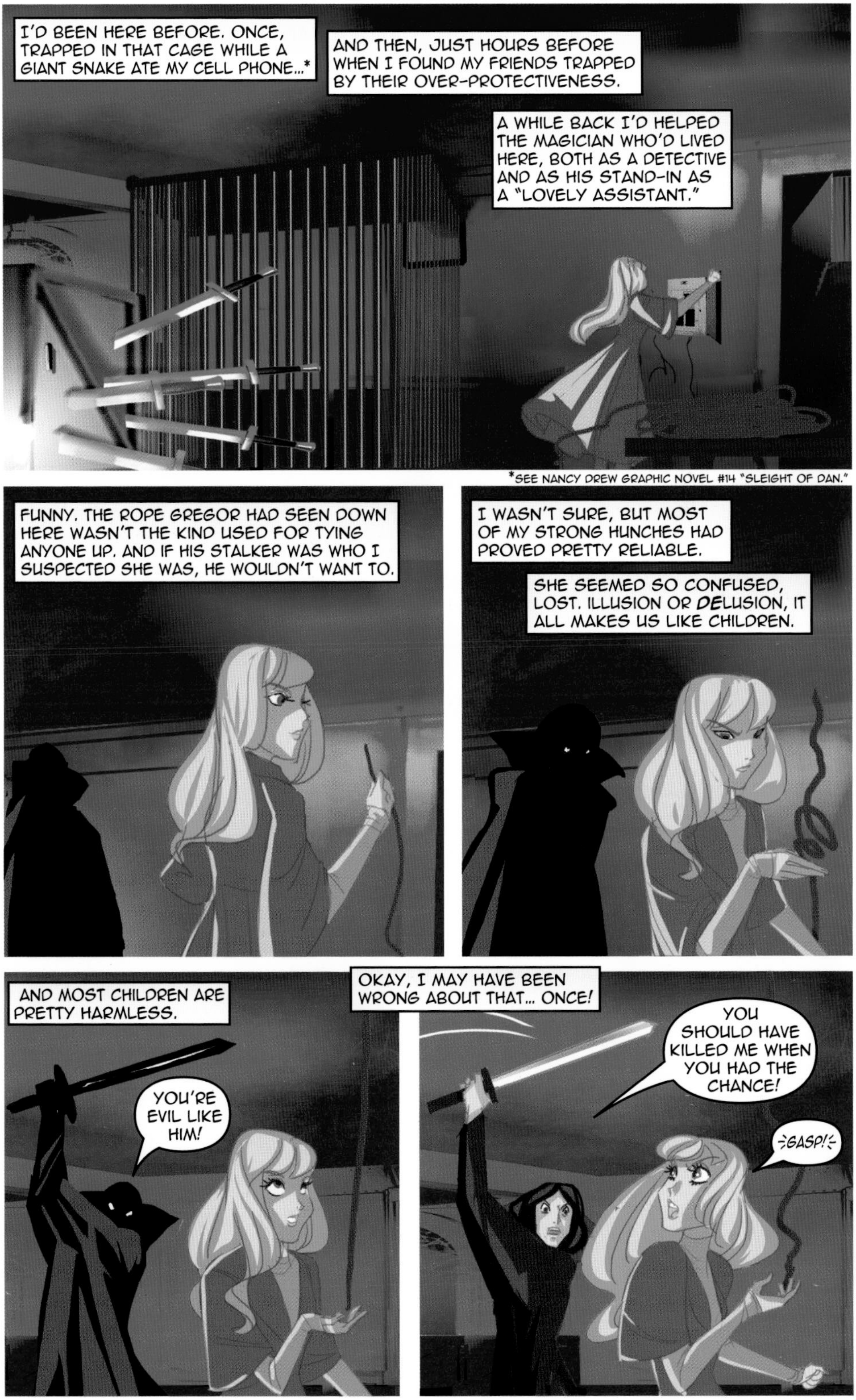
I'D BEEN HERE BEFORE. ONCE, TRAPPED IN THAT CAGE WHILE A GIANT SNAKE ATE MY CELL PHONE...*
AND THEN, JUST HOURS BEFORE WHEN I FOUND MY FRIENDS TRAPPED BY THEIR OVER-PROTECTIVENESS.
A WHILE BACK I'D HELPED THE MAGICIAN WHO'D LIVED HERE, BOTH AS A DETECTIVE AND AS HIS STAND-IN AS A "LOVELY ASSISTANT."
*SEE NANCY DREW GRAPHIC NOVEL #14 "SLEIGHT OF DAN."
FUNNY. THE ROPE GREGOR HAD SEEN DOWN HERE WASN'T THE KIND USED FOR TYING ANYONE UP. AND IF HIS STALKER WAS WHO I SUSPECTED SHE WAS, HE WOULDN'T WANT TO.
I WASN'T SURE, BUT MOST OF MY STRONG HUNCHES HAD PROVED PRETTY RELIABLE.
SHE SEEMED SO CONFUSED, LOST. ILLUSION OR *DE*LUSION, IT ALL MAKES US LIKE CHILDREN.
AND MOST CHILDREN ARE PRETTY HARMLESS.
YOU'RE EVIL LIKE HIM!
OKAY, I MAY HAVE BEEN WRONG ABOUT THAT... ONCE!
YOU SHOULD HAVE KILLED ME WHEN YOU HAD THE CHANCE!
GASP!

WHILE THE SITUATION WAS PRETTY DARK IN THE BASEMENT, THE SUN ROSE ON MY FRIENDS OUTSIDE, AS THEY GOT CLOSER TO FINDING THE KEYS TO MY FREEDOM!

BESS HAS ALWAYS HAD A MECHANICAL MIND.

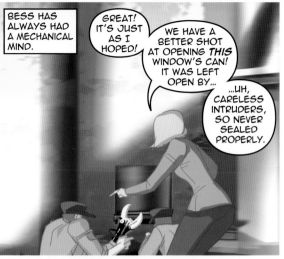

GREAT! IT'S JUST AS I HOPED!

WE HAVE A BETTER SHOT AT OPENING *THIS* WINDOW'S CAN! IT WAS LEFT OPEN BY...

...UH, CARELESS INTRUDERS, SO NEVER SEALED PROPERLY.

GEORGE IS THE COMPUTER GENIUS OF OUR DETECTIVE TEAM!

ON *MY* LAPTOP, I BROUGHT UP EACH OF THE ROOMS WHERE HE HAS CAMERAS.

BUT I DON'T SEE NANCY OR THE OTHER TWO YET! THEY'RE STILL MISSING.

NED? WELL, WHILE HE HASN'T HELPED ON *EVERY* CASE -- I JUST DON'T KNOW WHAT I'D DO WITHOUT HIM.

MEANWHILE, YOUR COMPUTER IS SCANNING FOR THE CODES TO SHUT THE SECURITY SYSTEM DOWN AND GET THOSE SHIELDS OPEN.

GOOD WORK! BUT, JUST FOR THE RECORD, THIS NEVER HAPPENED... ESPECIALLY IN MY CAR!

OF COURSE NOT!

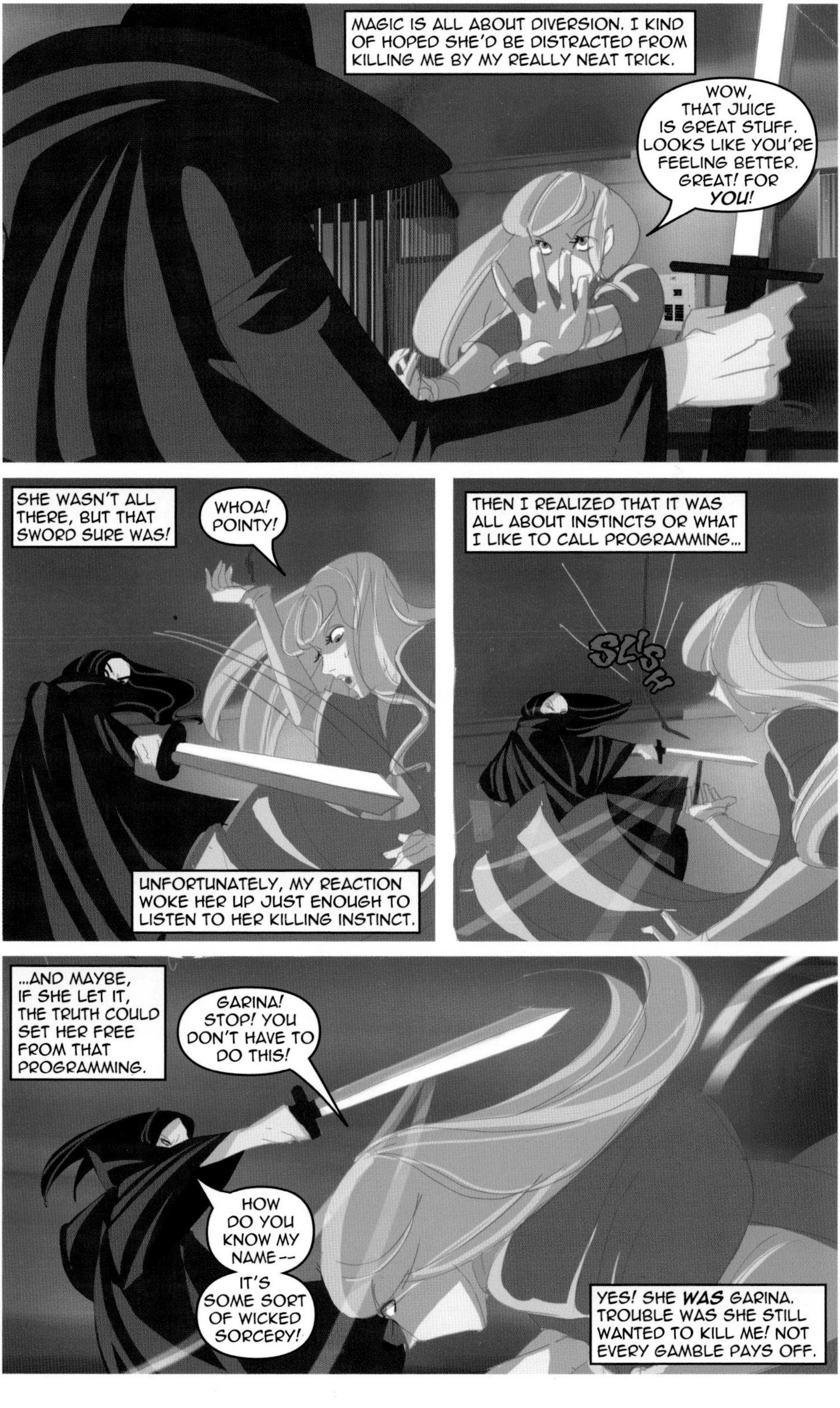
MAGIC IS ALL ABOUT DIVERSION. I KIND OF HOPED SHE'D BE DISTRACTED FROM KILLING ME BY MY REALLY NEAT TRICK.
WOW, THAT JUICE IS GREAT STUFF. LOOKS LIKE YOU'RE FEELING BETTER. GREAT! FOR *YOU*!
SHE WASN'T ALL THERE, BUT THAT SWORD SURE WAS!
WHOA! POINTY!
UNFORTUNATELY, MY REACTION WOKE HER UP JUST ENOUGH TO LISTEN TO HER KILLING INSTINCT.
THEN I REALIZED THAT IT WAS ALL ABOUT INSTINCTS OR WHAT I LIKE TO CALL PROGRAMMING...
SLISH
...AND MAYBE, IF SHE LET IT, THE TRUTH COULD SET HER FREE FROM THAT PROGRAMMING.
GARINA! STOP! YOU DON'T HAVE TO DO THIS!
HOW DO YOU KNOW MY NAME--
IT'S SOME SORT OF WICKED SORCERY!
YES! SHE *WAS* GARINA. TROUBLE WAS SHE STILL WANTED TO KILL ME! NOT EVERY GAMBLE PAYS OFF.

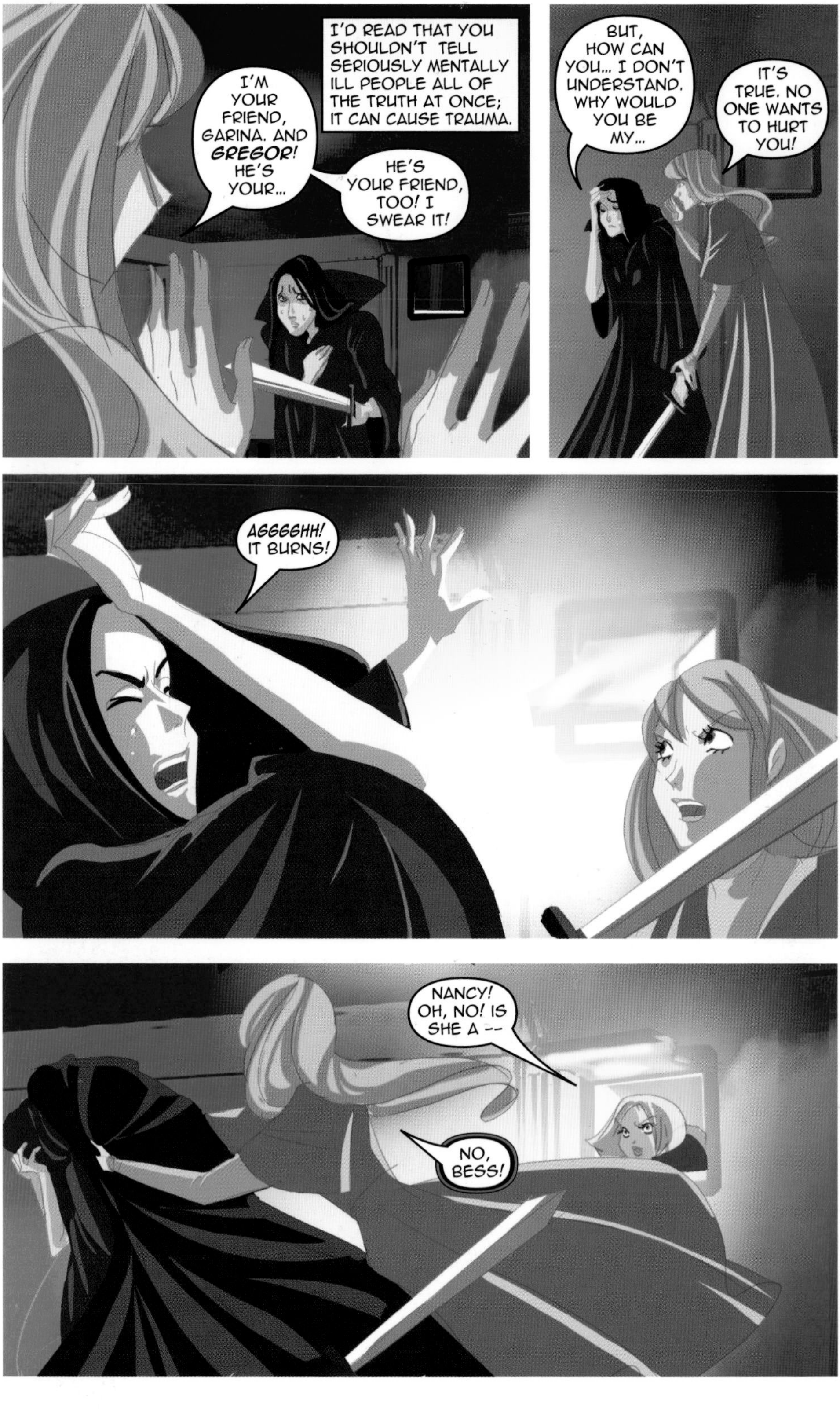
I'D READ THAT YOU SHOULDN'T TELL SERIOUSLY MENTALLY ILL PEOPLE ALL OF THE TRUTH AT ONCE; IT CAN CAUSE TRAUMA.
I'M YOUR FRIEND, GARINA. AND GREGOR! HE'S YOUR...
HE'S YOUR FRIEND, TOO! I SWEAR IT!
BUT, HOW CAN YOU... I DON'T UNDERSTAND. WHY WOULD YOU BE MY...
IT'S TRUE. NO ONE WANTS TO HURT YOU!
AGGGGHH! IT BURNS!
NANCY! OH, NO! IS SHE A --
NO, BESS!

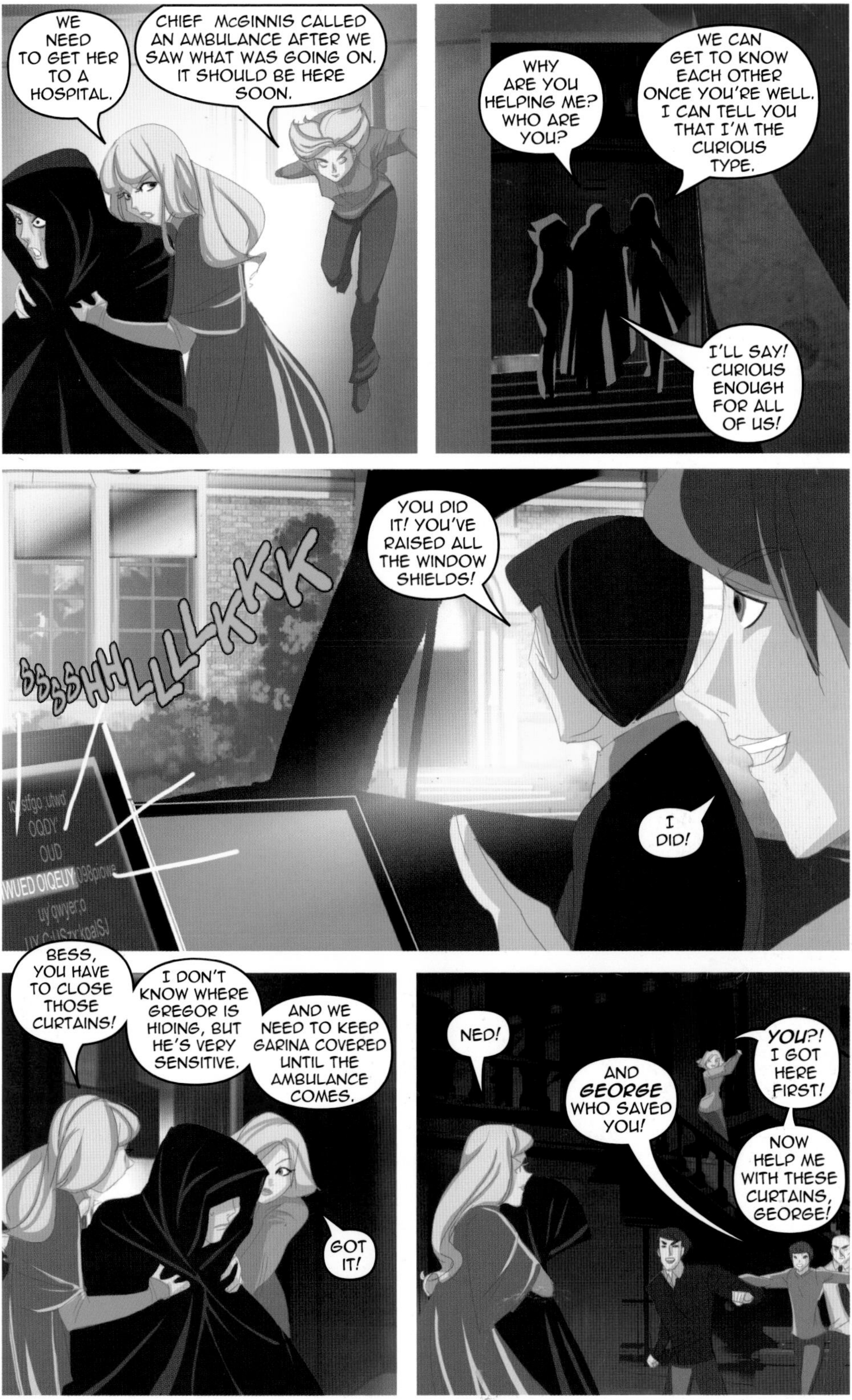
WE NEED TO GET HER TO A HOSPITAL.
CHIEF McGINNIS CALLED AN AMBULANCE AFTER WE SAW WHAT WAS GOING ON. IT SHOULD BE HERE SOON.
WHY ARE YOU HELPING ME? WHO ARE YOU?
WE CAN GET TO KNOW EACH OTHER ONCE YOU'RE WELL. I CAN TELL YOU THAT I'M THE CURIOUS TYPE.
I'LL SAY! CURIOUS ENOUGH FOR ALL OF US!
SSSSHHLLLLKKK
YOU DID IT! YOU'VE RAISED ALL THE WINDOW SHIELDS!
I DID!
BESS, YOU HAVE TO CLOSE THOSE CURTAINS!
I DON'T KNOW WHERE GREGOR IS HIDING, BUT HE'S VERY SENSITIVE.
AND WE NEED TO KEEP GARINA COVERED UNTIL THE AMBULANCE COMES.
GOT IT!
NED!
AND GEORGE WHO SAVED YOU!
YOU?! I GOT HERE FIRST!
NOW HELP ME WITH THESE CURTAINS, GEORGE!

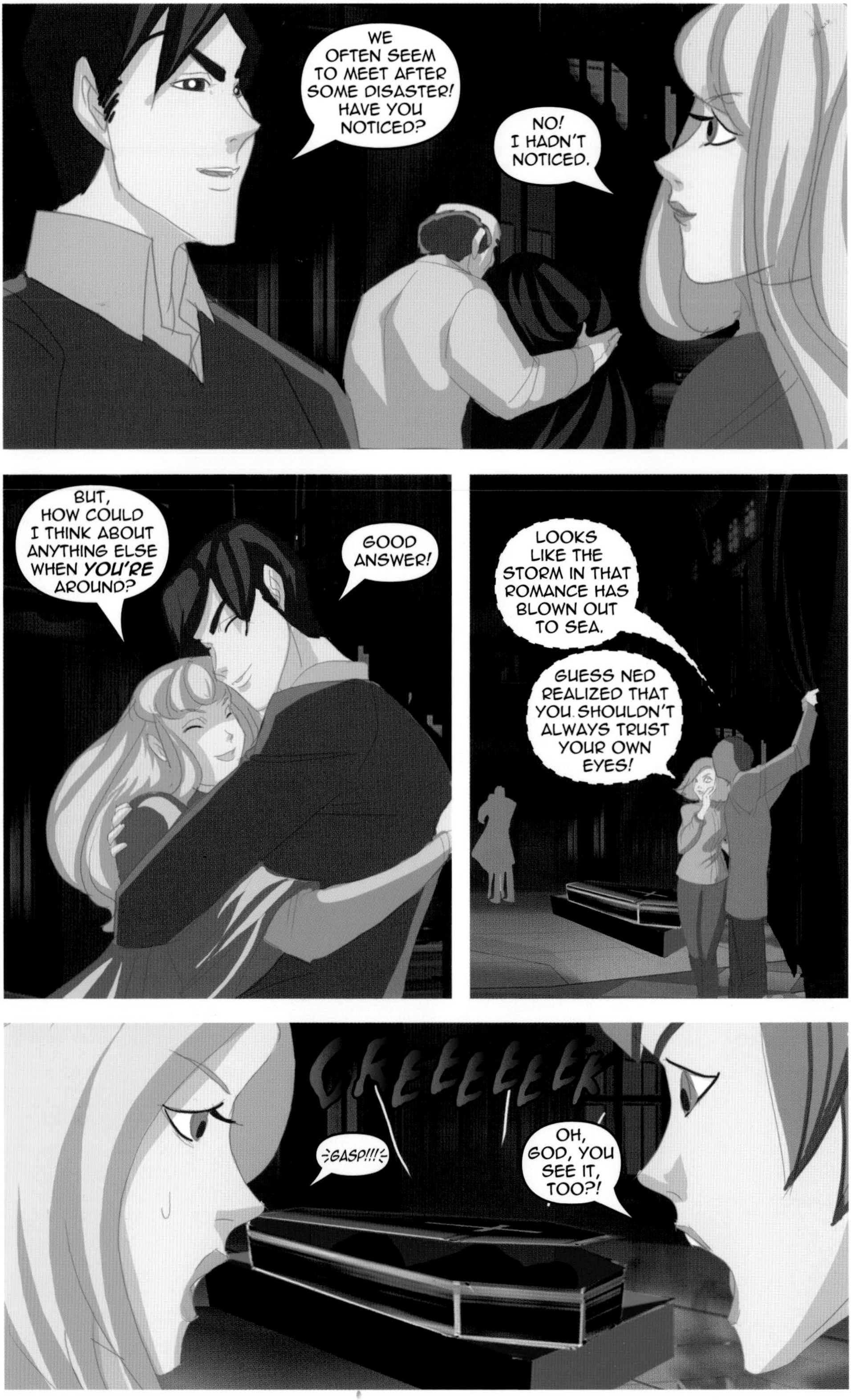
WE OFTEN SEEM TO MEET AFTER SOME DISASTER! HAVE YOU NOTICED?
NO! I HADN'T NOTICED.
BUT, HOW COULD I THINK ABOUT ANYTHING ELSE WHEN *YOU'RE* AROUND?
GOOD ANSWER!
LOOKS LIKE THE STORM IN THAT ROMANCE HAS BLOWN OUT TO SEA.
GUESS NED REALIZED THAT YOU SHOULDN'T ALWAYS TRUST YOUR OWN EYES!
GREEEEEER
GASP!!!
OH, GOD, YOU SEE IT, TOO?!

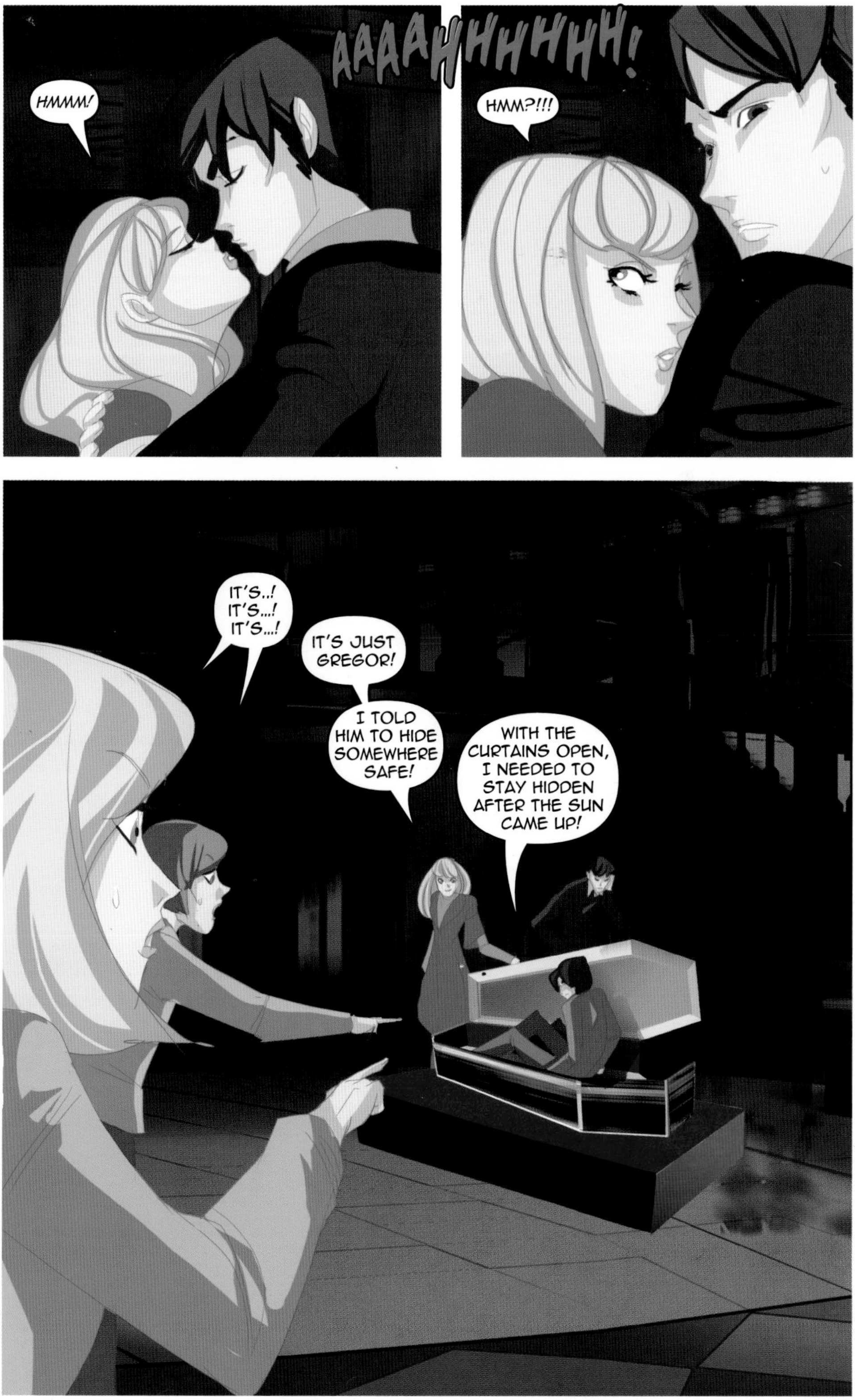
HMMM!
AAAAHHHHHH!
HMM?!!!
IT'S..!
IT'S...!
IT'S...!
IT'S JUST GREGOR!
I TOLD HIM TO HIDE SOMEWHERE SAFE!
WITH THE CURTAINS OPEN, I NEEDED TO STAY HIDDEN AFTER THE SUN CAME UP!

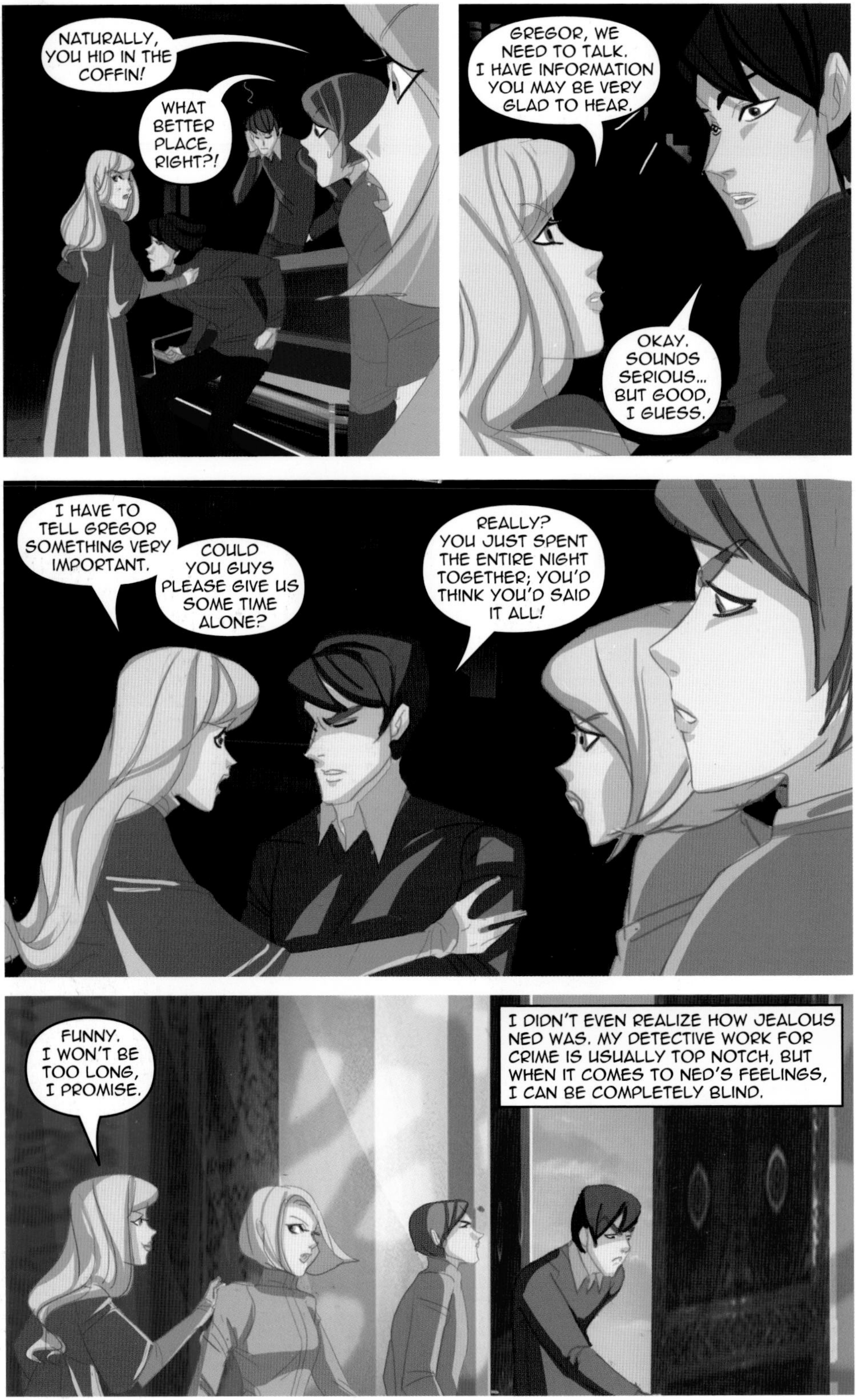
NATURALLY, YOU HID IN THE COFFIN!
WHAT BETTER PLACE, RIGHT?!
GREGOR, WE NEED TO TALK. I HAVE INFORMATION YOU MAY BE VERY GLAD TO HEAR.
OKAY. SOUNDS SERIOUS... BUT GOOD, I GUESS.
I HAVE TO TELL GREGOR SOMETHING VERY IMPORTANT.
COULD YOU GUYS PLEASE GIVE US SOME TIME ALONE?
REALLY? YOU JUST SPENT THE ENTIRE NIGHT TOGETHER; YOU'D THINK YOU'D SAID IT ALL!
FUNNY. I WON'T BE TOO LONG, I PROMISE.
I DIDN'T EVEN REALIZE HOW JEALOUS NED WAS. MY DETECTIVE WORK FOR CRIME IS USUALLY TOP NOTCH, BUT WHEN IT COMES TO NED'S FEELINGS, I CAN BE COMPLETELY BLIND.

I TOLD GREGOR THAT HIS STALKER'S NAME WAS GARINA AND IT WAS LIKELY THAT SHE WAS HIS TWIN SISTER.

WHO KNOWS HOW WELL HER PORPHYRIA'S BEEN TREATED. THEY'RE TAKING HER TO THE HOSPITAL.

I THINK YOU SHOULD GO AND TALK TO THE DOCTORS. MAYBE TALK TO HER.

I CAN'T BELIEVE THIS. YOU'RE LIKE SOME BRIGHT ANGEL IN MY DARK WORLD, NANCY DREW.

MY WHOLE LIFE HAS CHANGED, BECAUSE OF *YOU*. YOU MAKE THE PAIN, THE LONELINESS... DISAPPEAR!

I KNOW I CAN FACE THE HEALING AHEAD WITH YOU BY MY SIDE, NANCY DREW!

GREGOR, I--

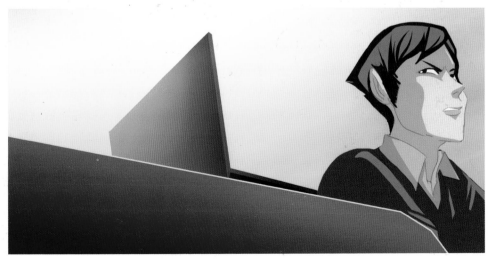

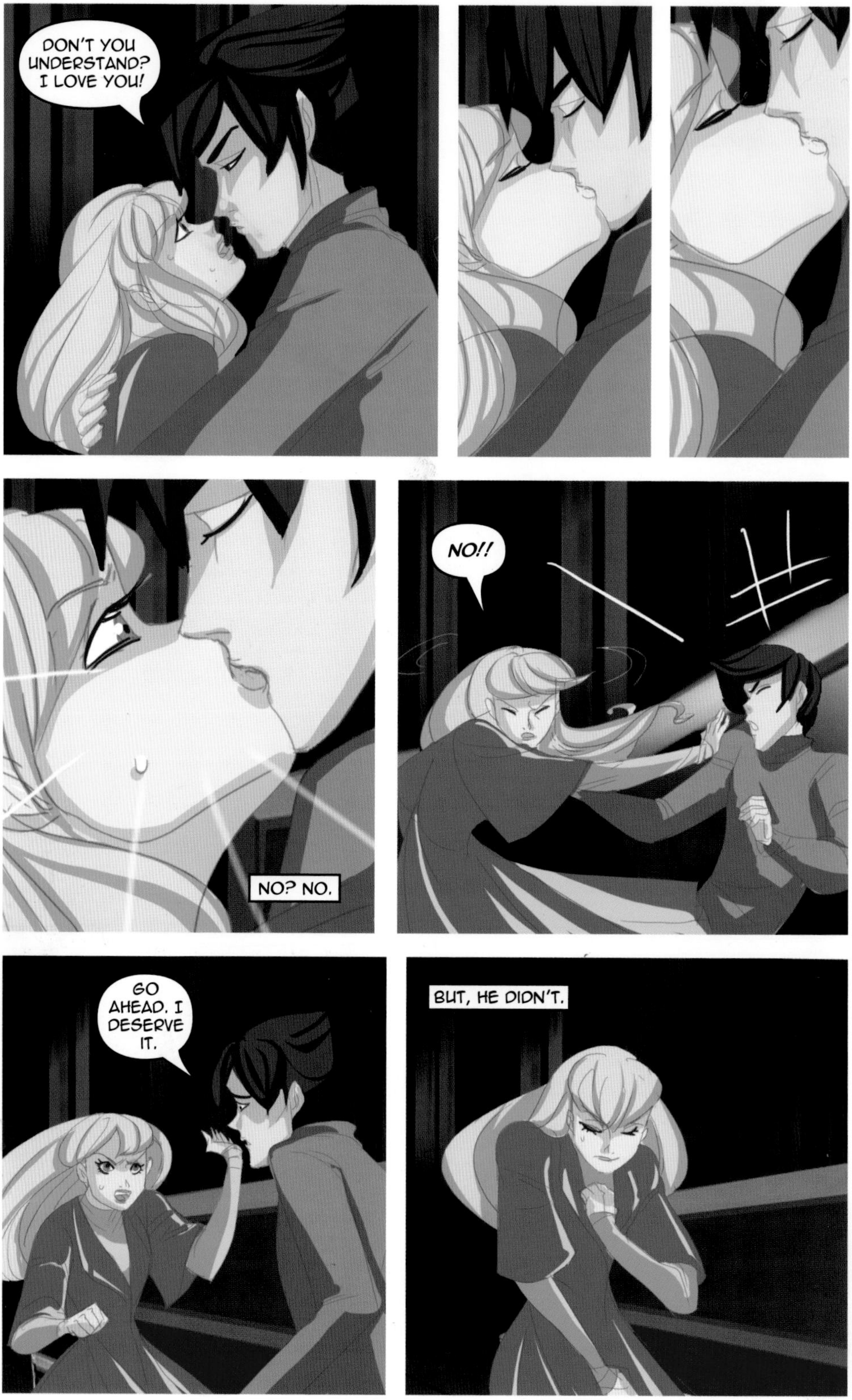
DON'T YOU UNDERSTAND? I LOVE YOU!
NO? NO.
NO!!
GO AHEAD. I DESERVE IT.
BUT, HE DIDN'T.

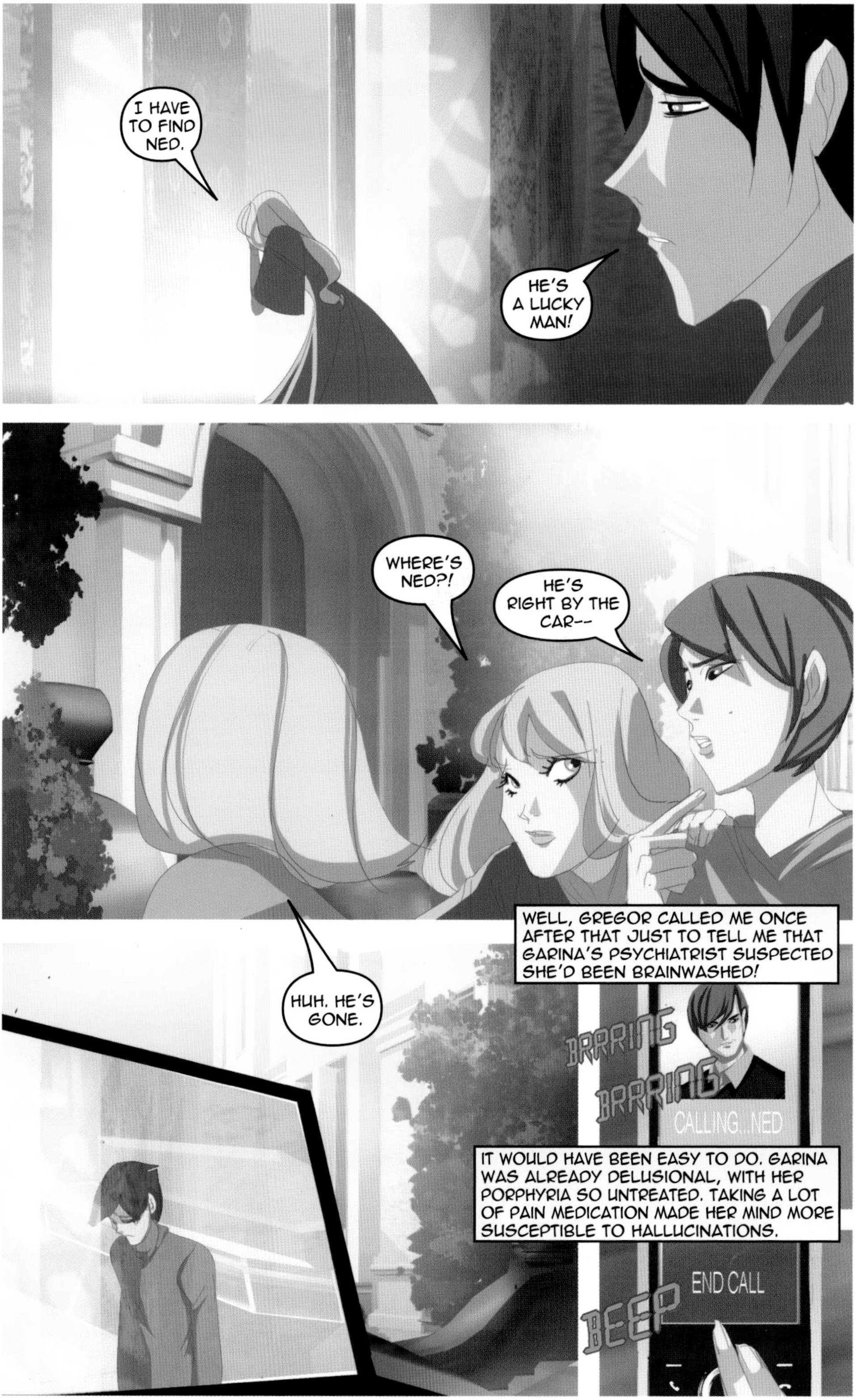
I HAVE TO FIND NED.
HE'S A LUCKY MAN!
WHERE'S NED?!
HE'S RIGHT BY THE CAR--
HUH. HE'S GONE.
WELL, GREGOR CALLED ME ONCE AFTER THAT JUST TO TELL ME THAT GARINA'S PSYCHIATRIST SUSPECTED SHE'D BEEN BRAINWASHED!
BRRRING
BRRRING
CALLING...NED
IT WOULD HAVE BEEN EASY TO DO. GARINA WAS ALREADY DELUSIONAL, WITH HER PORPHYRIA SO UNTREATED. TAKING A LOT OF PAIN MEDICATION MADE HER MIND MORE SUSCEPTIBLE TO HALLUCINATIONS.
END CALL
BEEP

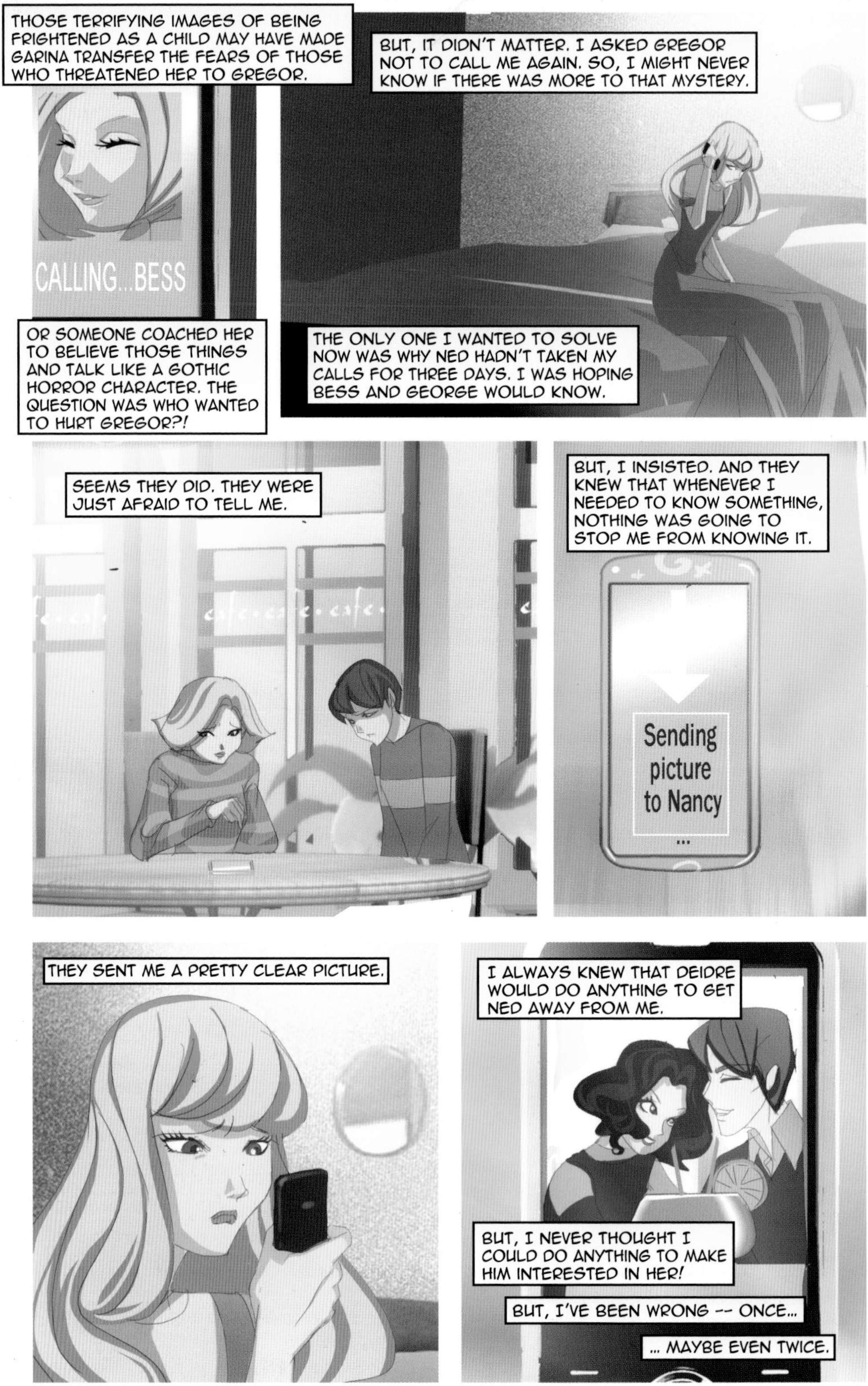
THOSE TERRIFYING IMAGES OF BEING FRIGHTENED AS A CHILD MAY HAVE MADE GARINA TRANSFER THE FEARS OF THOSE WHO THREATENED HER TO GREGOR.
CALLING...BESS
OR SOMEONE COACHED HER TO BELIEVE THOSE THINGS AND TALK LIKE A GOTHIC HORROR CHARACTER. THE QUESTION WAS WHO WANTED TO HURT GREGOR?!
BUT, IT DIDN'T MATTER. I ASKED GREGOR NOT TO CALL ME AGAIN. SO, I MIGHT NEVER KNOW IF THERE WAS MORE TO THAT MYSTERY.
THE ONLY ONE I WANTED TO SOLVE NOW WAS WHY NED HADN'T TAKEN MY CALLS FOR THREE DAYS. I WAS HOPING BESS AND GEORGE WOULD KNOW.
SEEMS THEY DID. THEY WERE JUST AFRAID TO TELL ME.
BUT, I INSISTED. AND THEY KNEW THAT WHENEVER I NEEDED TO KNOW SOMETHING, NOTHING WAS GOING TO STOP ME FROM KNOWING IT.
Sending picture to Nancy
...
THEY SENT ME A PRETTY CLEAR PICTURE.
I ALWAYS KNEW THAT DEIDRE WOULD DO ANYTHING TO GET NED AWAY FROM ME.
BUT, I NEVER THOUGHT I COULD DO ANYTHING TO MAKE HIM INTERESTED IN HER!
BUT, I'VE BEEN WRONG -- ONCE...
... MAYBE EVEN TWICE.

NANCY DREW GRAPHIC NOVELS AVAILABLE FROM PAPERCUTZ

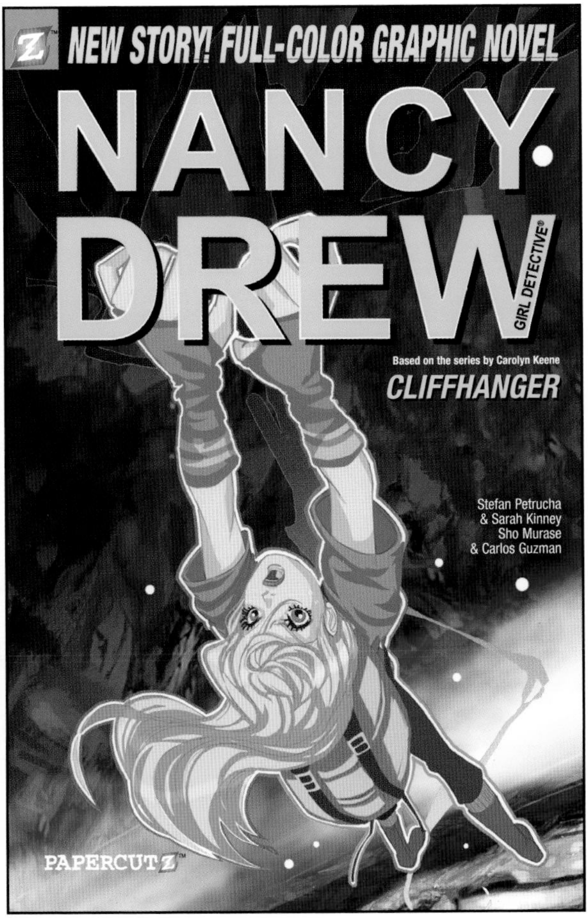

NEW STORY! FULL-COLOR GRAPHIC NOVEL
NANCY DREW
GIRL DETECTIVE®
Based on the series by Carolyn Keene
CLIFFHANGER
Stefan Petrucha
& Sarah Kinney
Sho Murase
& Carlos Guzman
PAPERCUTZ

#19 "Cliffhanger"

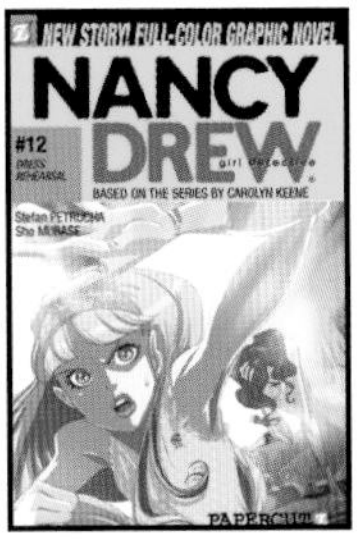

NEW STORY! FULL-COLOR GRAPHIC NOVEL
NANCY DREW
girl detective
#12
BASED ON THE SERIES BY CAROLYN KEENE
Stefan Petrucha
Sho Murase
PAPERCUTZ

#12 "Dress Reversal"

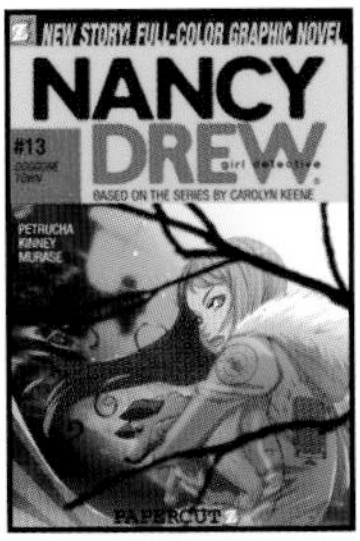

NEW STORY! FULL-COLOR GRAPHIC NOVEL
NANCY DREW
girl detective
#13
BASED ON THE SERIES BY CAROLYN KEENE
PETRUCHA
KINNEY
MURASE
PAPERCUTZ

#13 "Doggone Town"

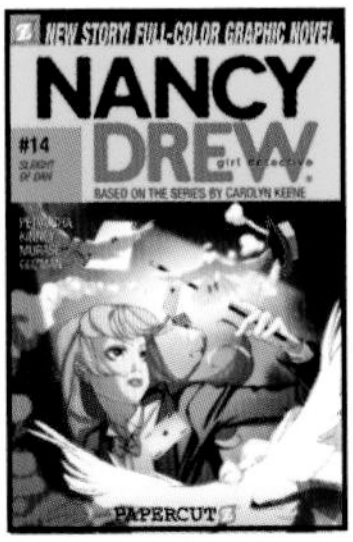

NEW STORY! FULL-COLOR GRAPHIC NOVEL
NANCY DREW
girl detective
#14
BASED ON THE SERIES BY CAROLYN KEENE
PAPERCUTZ

#14 "Sleight of Dan"

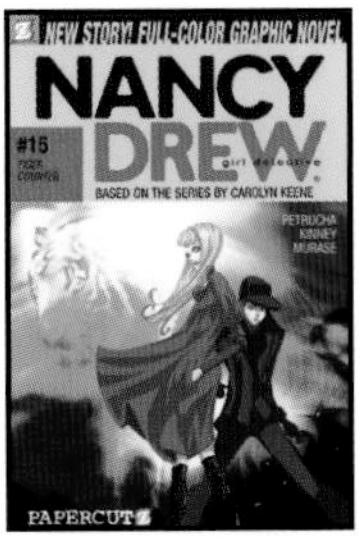

NEW STORY! FULL-COLOR GRAPHIC NOVEL
NANCY DREW
girl detective
#15
BASED ON THE SERIES BY CAROLYN KEENE
PETRUCHA
KINNEY
MURASE
PAPERCUTZ

#15 "Tiger Counter"

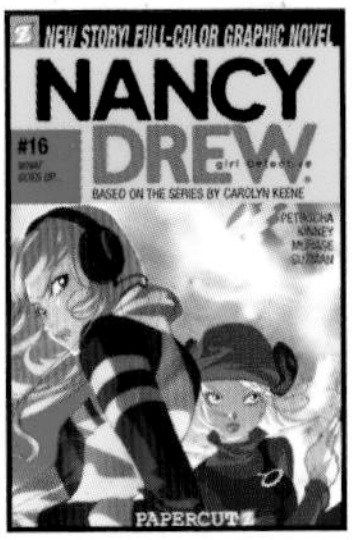

NEW STORY! FULL-COLOR GRAPHIC NOVEL
NANCY DREW
girl detective
#16
BASED ON THE SERIES BY CAROLYN KEENE
PETRUCHA
KINNEY
MURASE
GUZMAN
PAPERCUTZ

#16 "What Goes Up..."

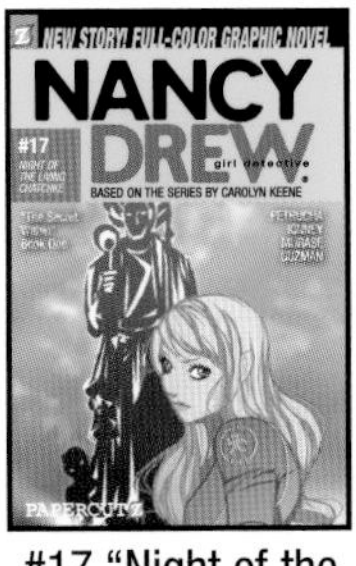

NEW STORY! FULL-COLOR GRAPHIC NOVEL
NANCY DREW
girl detective
#17
BASED ON THE SERIES BY CAROLYN KEENE
PETRUCHA
KINNEY
MURASE
GUZMAN
PAPERCUTZ

#17 "Night of the Living Chatchke"

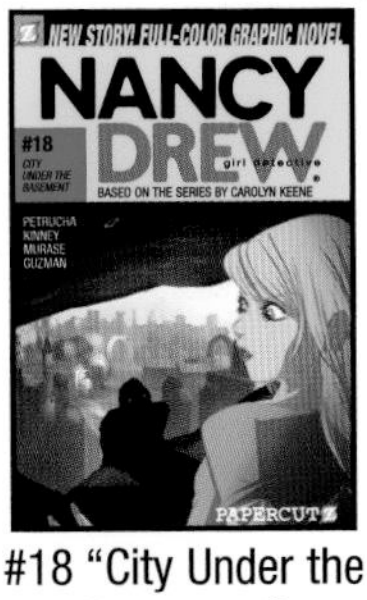

NEW STORY! FULL-COLOR GRAPHIC NOVEL
NANCY DREW
girl detective
#18
CITY UNDER THE BASEMENT
BASED ON THE SERIES BY CAROLYN KEENE
PETRUCHA
KINNEY
MURASE
GUZMAN
PAPERCUTZ

#18 "City Under the Basement"

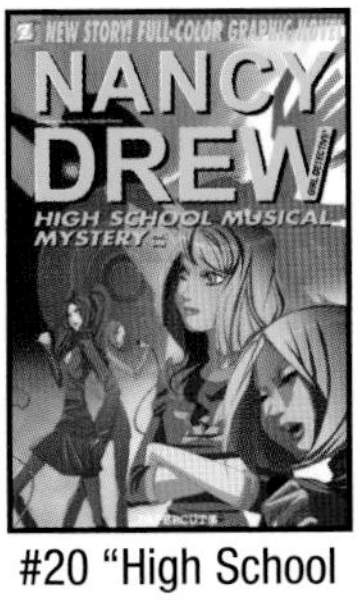

NEW STORY! FULL-COLOR GRAPHIC NOVEL
NANCY DREW
HIGH SCHOOL MUSICAL MYSTERY

#20 "High School Musical Mystery" 1

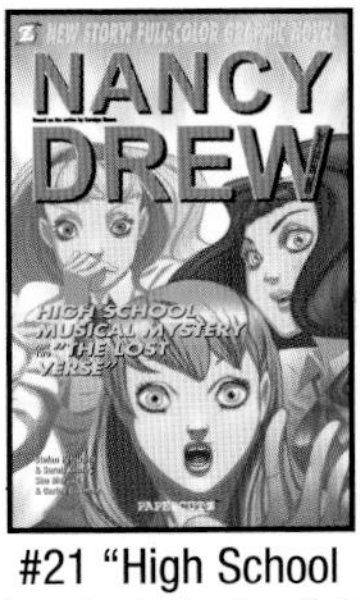

NEW STORY! FULL-COLOR GRAPHIC NOVEL
NANCY DREW
HIGH SCHOOL MUSICAL MYSTERY
"THE LOST VERSE"

#21 "High School Musical Mystery" 2

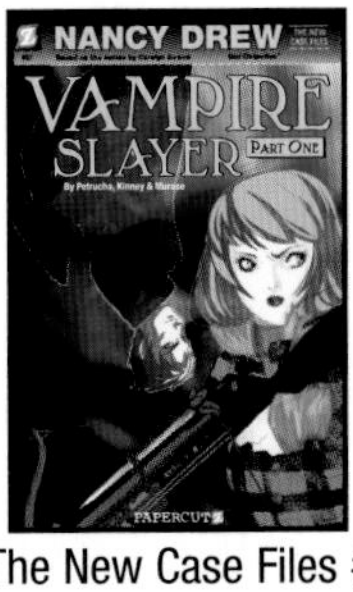

NANCY DREW
VAMPIRE SLAYER PART ONE
By Petrucha, Kinney & Murase
PAPERCUTZ

The New Case Files #1 "Vampire Slayer" Part 1

Graphic Novels #12-19 are $7.95 in paperback, $12.95 hardcover. Graphic Novels #20 and #21 are $8.99 in paperback, $13.99 hardcover. NANCY DREW The New Case Files #1 is $6.99 in paperback, $10.99 hardcover. Please add $4.00 for postage and handling for the first book, add $1.00 for each additional book.

Please make check payable to NBM Publishing. Send to:

Papercutz, 1200 County Rd. Rte. 523, Flemington, NJ 08822, 1-800-886-1223

www.papercutz.com

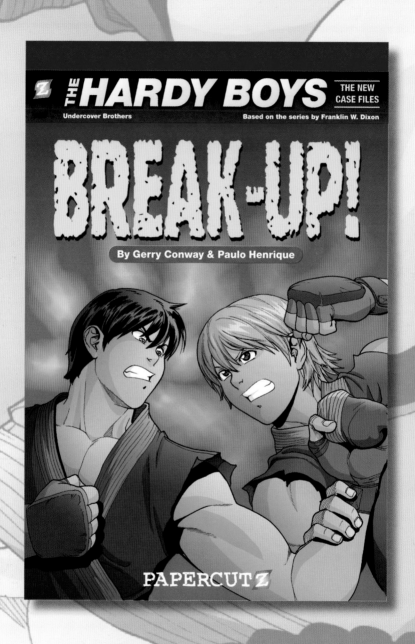

WATCH OUT FOR PAPERCUTZ ™

Welcome to the second edition of the all-new NANCY DREW graphic novel series! I'm Jim Salicrup, Editor-in-Chief of Papercutz, publisher of graphic novels for all-ages. If you picked up NANCY DREW The New Case Files #1, welcome back! If you're new to Nancy Drew comics, well, get ready for an exciting adventure featuring your favorite Girl Detective and all her friends (and a few frenemies) from her prose series. And if you're a total Nancy Drew newbie—then you're about to meet the Girl Detective who has thrilled generations of fans with her sleuthing skills, and her insatiable desire to solve mysteries. I suspect you'll soon be falling in love with Nancy Drew too!

Speaking of loving Nancy Drew, (SPOILER ALERT—skip to next paragraph if you haven't yet read "Vampire Slayer" Part Two!), what do you think of the surprising developments in the chilling conclusion to "Vampire Slayer"?! Did you ever think you'd see anyone other than Ned Nickerson kissing Nancy Drew? And what about Ned hooking up with Deirdre Shannon…? Obviously there's a lot of unexpected events going on in River Heights these days, and that leads us to the news many of you have been waiting for ever since Nancy Drew first appeared in her own series of graphic novels! Read on…

If you picked up THE HARDY BOYS The New Case Files #1 "Crawling with Zombies" or #2 "Break Up!" then you'll know that strange things have also been happening in the town of Bayport! First, Undercover Brothers Frank and Joe Hardy encounter a bizarre plot involving teens disguised as zombies, and as a result of conflicting crime-fighting styles, the two A.T.A.C. (American Teens Against Crime) agents decide they no longer want to work together! How unbelievable is that?! The Hardy Boys have been a team—like forever! Can they really being going their separate ways? Well, yes—and that leads us to our biggest announcement yet!

Frank and Joe Hardy are now convinced, based on all the clues they've uncovered, that the mastermind behind all the recent weirdness in Bayport is in the town of River Heights—and that they need to go there to find answers. And if you guessed that that means The Hardy Boys will be co-starring in NANCY DREW The New Case Files #3 "Together With The Hardy Boys," then you are correct!

Yes, it's true! Ever since we started publishing the Papercutz HARDY BOYS and NANCY DREW graphic novels, you have been demanding that we publish an adventure with Frank, Joe, and Nancy together! We held out because we really wanted to make it something extra-special! After all, The Hardys and Miss Drew have worked together numerous times in books and on TV in the past, and we wanted to do something a little different. This time, Nancy is caught between Frank and Joe Hardy, who no longer want to work together, (ANOTHER SPOILER WARNING! Skip to next paragraph if you haven't yet read "Vampire Slayer" Part Two!) at a time when she may be split with Ned! Maybe we should've titled NANCY DREW The New Case Files #3 "It's Complicated!"

As exciting as that HARDY BOYS/NANCY DREW bombshell may be—there's still other amazing graphic novels being published by Papercutz as well! You may've heard about an all-new, blockbuster 3-D Smurfs movie coming to a theater near you August 3rd, 2011, or maybe you enjoy the Smurfs cartoons on the Boomerang channel! But did you know that the Smurfs first appeared in comics? They were created by the great cartoonist Peyo, and Papercutz is proud to now be publishing those classic comics in THE SMURFS graphic novels! To get a small sample of smurfy goodness, just check out the next few pages for a preview of THE SMURFS Graphic Novel #3 "The Smurf King"! You may be surprised to discover that it's more sophisticated than you might have thought! Be sure to check out the whole story, and enjoy the satire and fun.

That's more than enough for now. So, until next time—keep sleuthing!

Special Smurfy Preview of THE SMURFS Graphic Novel #3 “The Smurf King”…

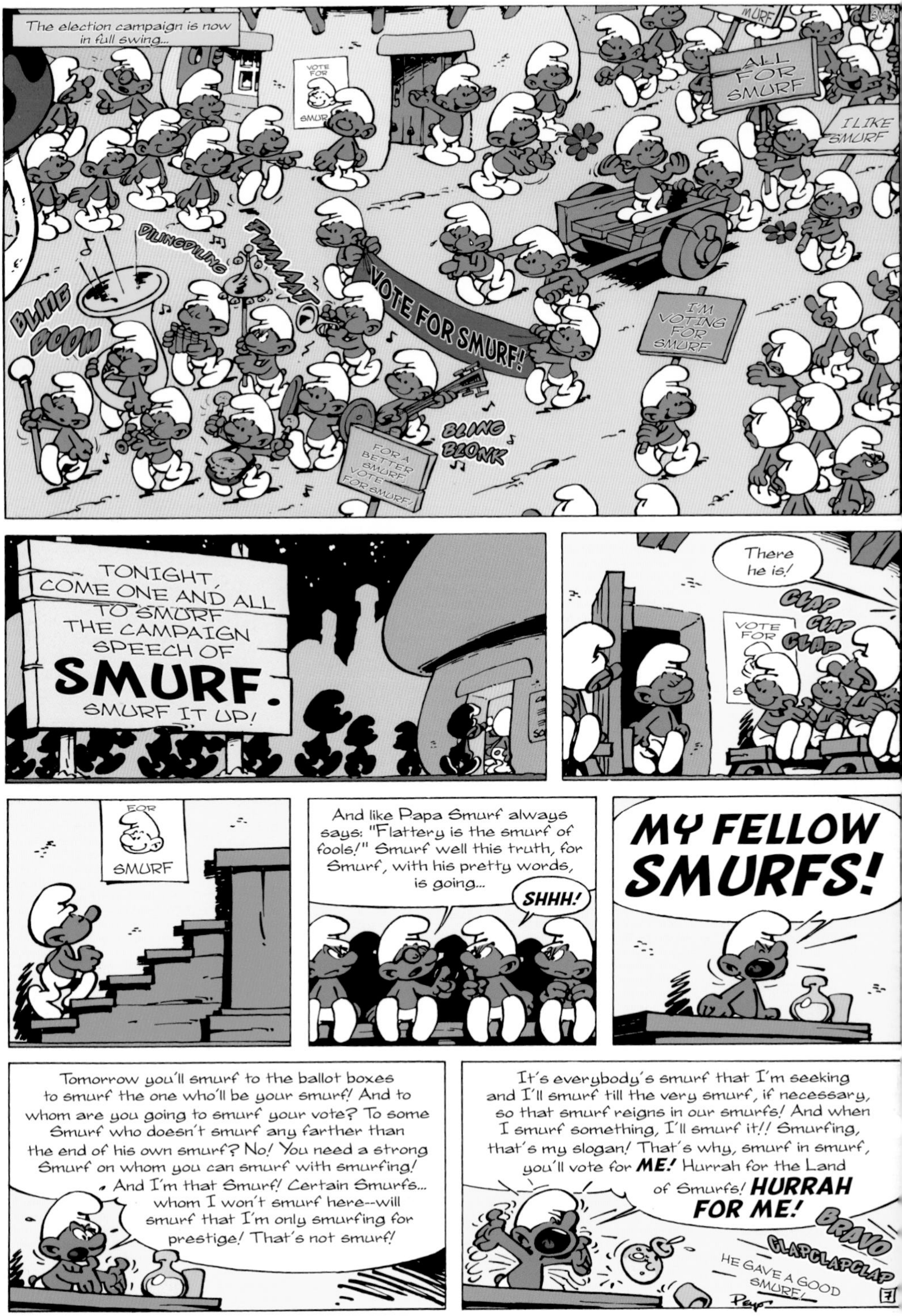
The election campaign is now in full swing...
VOTE FOR SMURF
SMURF
ALL FOR SMURF
I LIKE SMURF
DILINGDILING
PWAAAAT
BLING
BOOM
VOTE FOR SMURF!
I'M VOTING FOR SMURF
FOR A BETTER SMURF, VOTE FOR SMURF!
BLING
BLONK
TONIGHT, COME ONE AND ALL TO SMURF THE CAMPAIGN SPEECH OF SMURF. SMURF IT UP!
There he is!
CLAP
CLAP
CLAP
VOTE FOR
FOR
SMURF
And like Papa Smurf always says: "Flattery is the smurf of fools!" Smurf well this truth, for Smurf, with his pretty words, is going...
SHHH!
MY FELLOW SMURFS!
Tomorrow you'll smurf to the ballot boxes to smurf the one who'll be your smurf! And to whom are you going to smurf your vote? To some Smurf who doesn't smurf any farther than the end of his own smurf? No! You need a strong Smurf on whom you can smurf with smurfing!
And I'm that Smurf! Certain Smurfs... whom I won't smurf here--will smurf that I'm only smurfing for prestige! That's not smurf!
It's everybody's smurf that I'm seeking and I'll smurf till the very smurf, if necessary, so that smurf reigns in our smurfs! And when I smurf something, I'll smurf it!! Smurfing, that's my slogan! That's why, smurf in smurf, you'll vote for ME! Hurrah for the Land of Smurfs! HURRAH FOR ME!
BRAVO
CLAPCLAPCLAP
HE GAVE A GOOD SMURF!
7

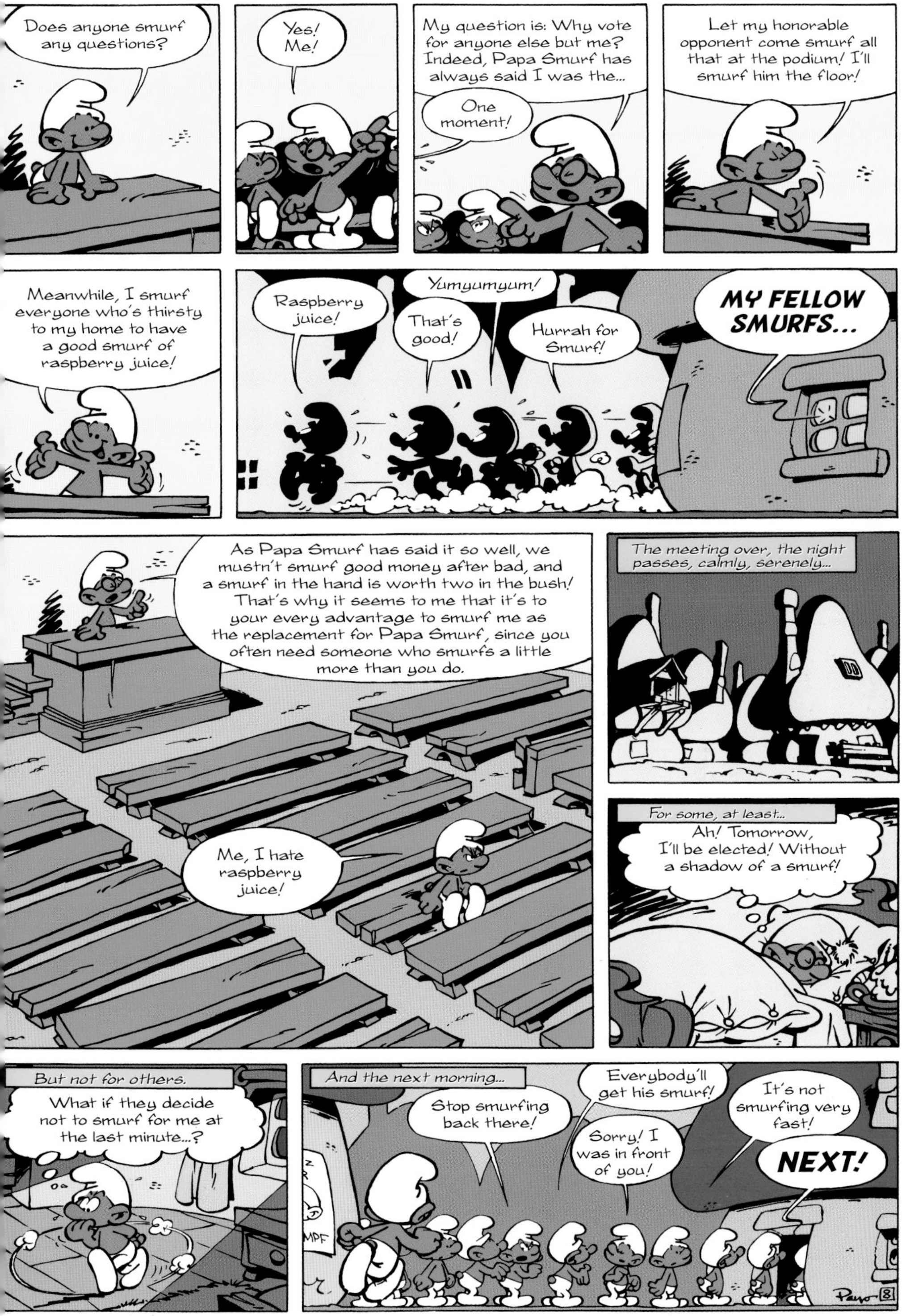
Does anyone smurf any questions?
Yes! Me!
My question is: Why vote for anyone else but me? Indeed, Papa Smurf has always said I was the...
One moment!
Let my honorable opponent come smurf all that at the podium! I'll smurf him the floor!
Meanwhile, I smurf everyone who's thirsty to my home to have a good smurf of raspberry juice!
Raspberry juice!
Yumyumyum!
That's good!
Hurrah for Smurf!
MY FELLOW SMURFS...
As Papa Smurf has said it so well, we mustn't smurf good money after bad, and a smurf in the hand is worth two in the bush! That's why it seems to me that it's to your every advantage to smurf me as the replacement for Papa Smurf, since you often need someone who smurfs a little more than you do.
Me, I hate raspberry juice!
The meeting over, the night passes, calmly, serenely...
For some, at least...
Ah! Tomorrow, I'll be elected! Without a shadow of a smurf!
But not for others.
What if they decide not to smurf for me at the last minute...?
And the next morning...
Stop smurfing back there!
Everybody'll get his smurf!
Sorry! I was in front of you!
It's not smurfing very fast!
NEXT!
8

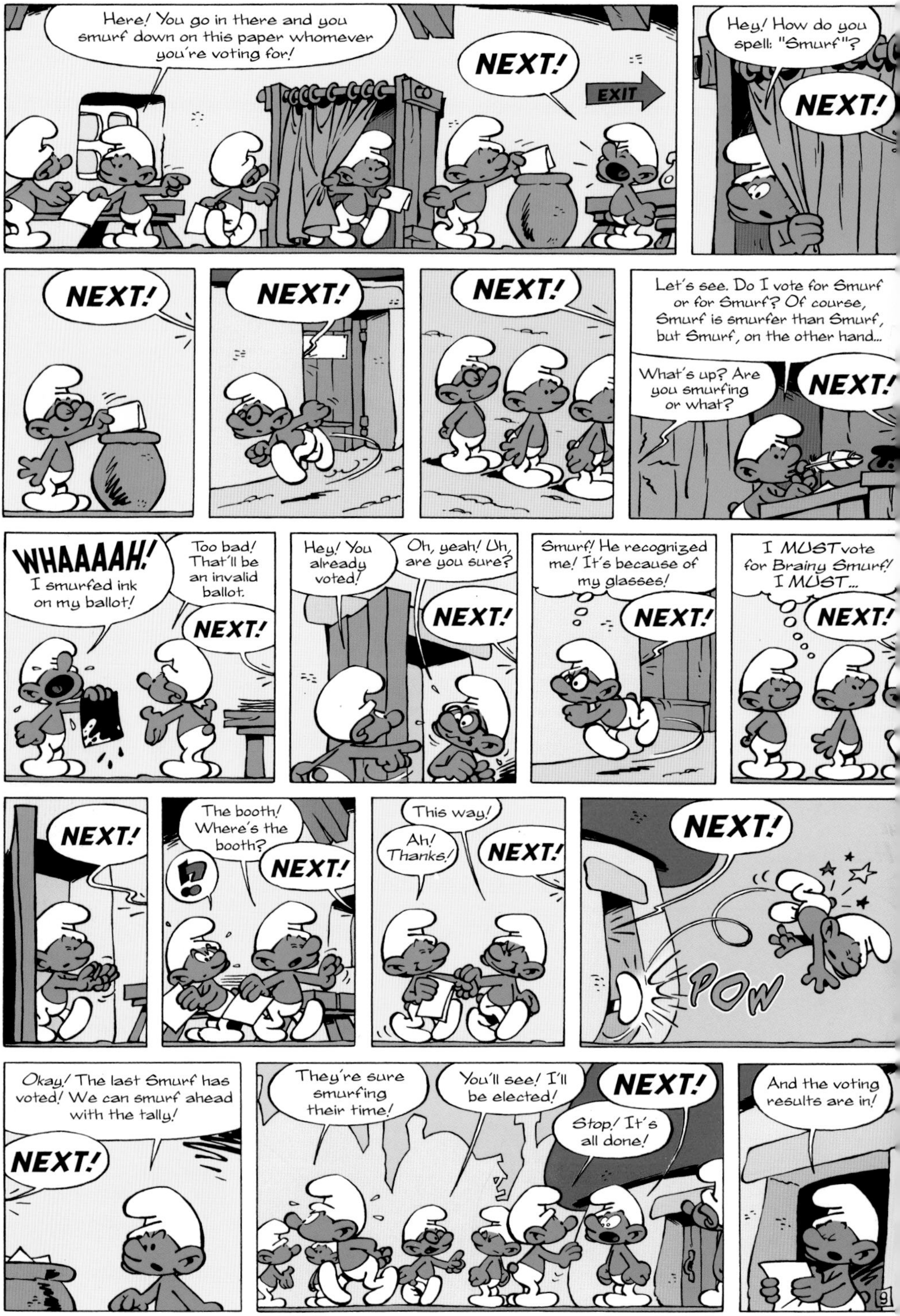
Here! You go in there and you smurf down on this paper whomever you're voting for!
NEXT!
EXIT
Hey! How do you spell: "Smurf"?
NEXT!
NEXT!
NEXT!
NEXT!
Let's see. Do I vote for Smurf or for Smurf? Of course, Smurf is smurfer than Smurf, but Smurf, on the other hand...
What's up? Are you smurfing or what?
NEXT!
WHAAAAH! I smurfed ink on my ballot!
Too bad! That'll be an invalid ballot.
NEXT!
Hey! You already voted!
Oh, yeah! Uh, are you sure?
NEXT!
Smurf! He recognized me! It's because of my glasses!
NEXT!
I MUST vote for Brainy Smurf! I MUST...
NEXT!
NEXT!
The booth! Where's the booth?
NEXT!
This way!
Ah! Thanks!
NEXT!
NEXT!
POW
Okay! The last Smurf has voted! We can smurf ahead with the tally!
NEXT!
They're sure smurfing their time!
You'll see! I'll be elected!
NEXT!
Stop! It's all done!
And the voting results are in!

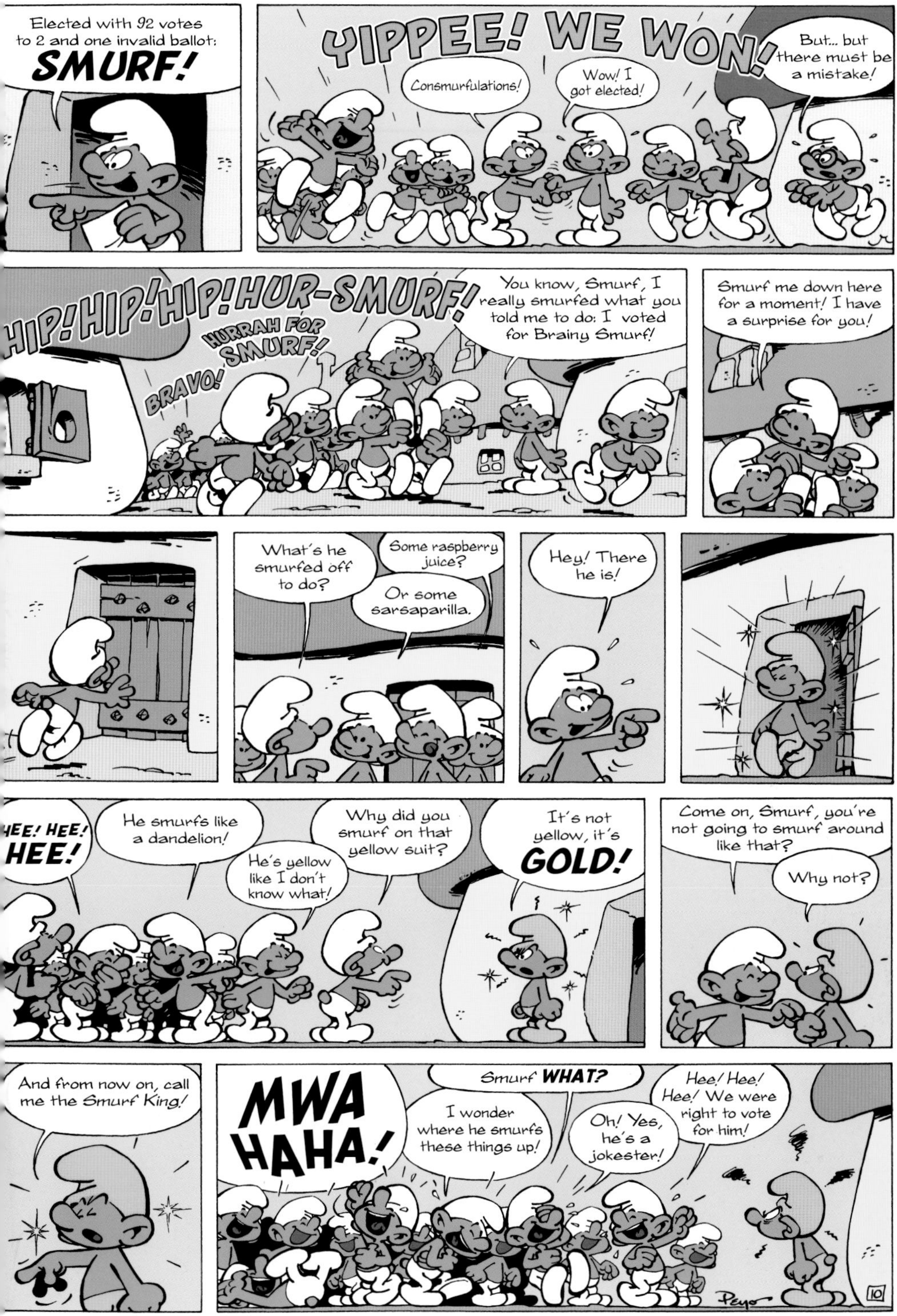
Elected with 92 votes to 2 and one invalid ballot: SMURF!
YIPPEE! WE WON!
Consmurfulations!
Wow! I got elected!
But... but there must be a mistake!
HIP! HIP! HIP! HUR-SMURF!
HURRAH FOR SMURF!
BRAVO!
You know, Smurf, I really smurfed what you told me to do: I voted for Brainy Smurf!
Smurf me down here for a moment! I have a surprise for you!
What's he smurfed off to do?
Some raspberry juice?
Or some sarsaparilla.
Hey! There he is!
HEE! HEE! HEE!
He smurfs like a dandelion!
He's yellow like I don't know what!
Why did you smurf on that yellow suit?
It's not yellow, it's GOLD!
Come on, Smurf, you're not going to smurf around like that?
Why not?
And from now on, call me the Smurf King!
MWA HAHA!
Smurf WHAT?
I wonder where he smurfs these things up!
Oh! Yes, he's a jokester!
Hee! Hee! Hee! We were right to vote for him!
Peyo
10

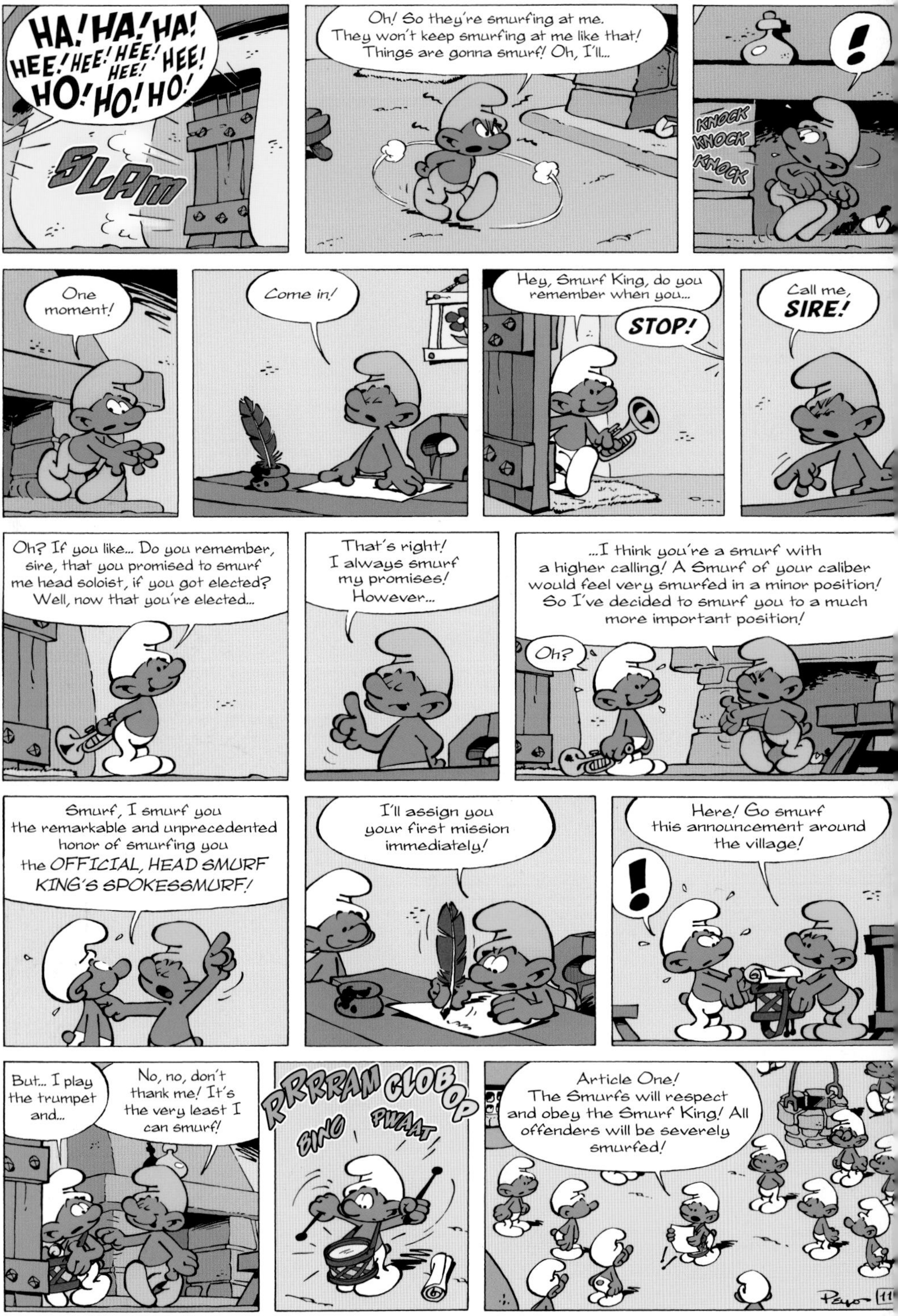
HA! HA! HA! HEE! HEE! HEE! HEE! HEE! HO! HO! HO!
SLAM
Oh! So they're smurfing at me. They won't keep smurfing at me like that! Things are gonna smurf! Oh, I'll...
!
KNOCK KNOCK KNOCK
One moment!
Come in!
Hey, Smurf King, do you remember when you...
STOP!
Call me, SIRE!
Oh? If you like... Do you remember, sire, that you promised to smurf me head soloist, if you got elected? Well, now that you're elected...
That's right! I always smurf my promises! However...
...I think you're a smurf with a higher calling! A Smurf of your caliber would feel very smurfed in a minor position! So I've decided to smurf you to a much more important position!
Oh?
Smurf, I smurf you the remarkable and unprecedented honor of smurfing you the OFFICIAL, HEAD SMURF KING'S SPOKESSMURF!
I'll assign you your first mission immediately!
Here! Go smurf this announcement around the village!
!
But... I play the trumpet and...
No, no, don't thank me! It's the very least I can smurf!
RRRRAM CLOBOP
BING PWAAT
Article One! The Smurfs will respect and obey the Smurf King! All offenders will be severely smurfed!
!
Peyo
11

Get the complete story in THE SMURFS Graphic Novel #3 "The Smurf King" available at booksellers everywhere!

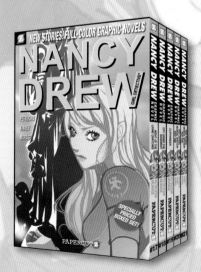

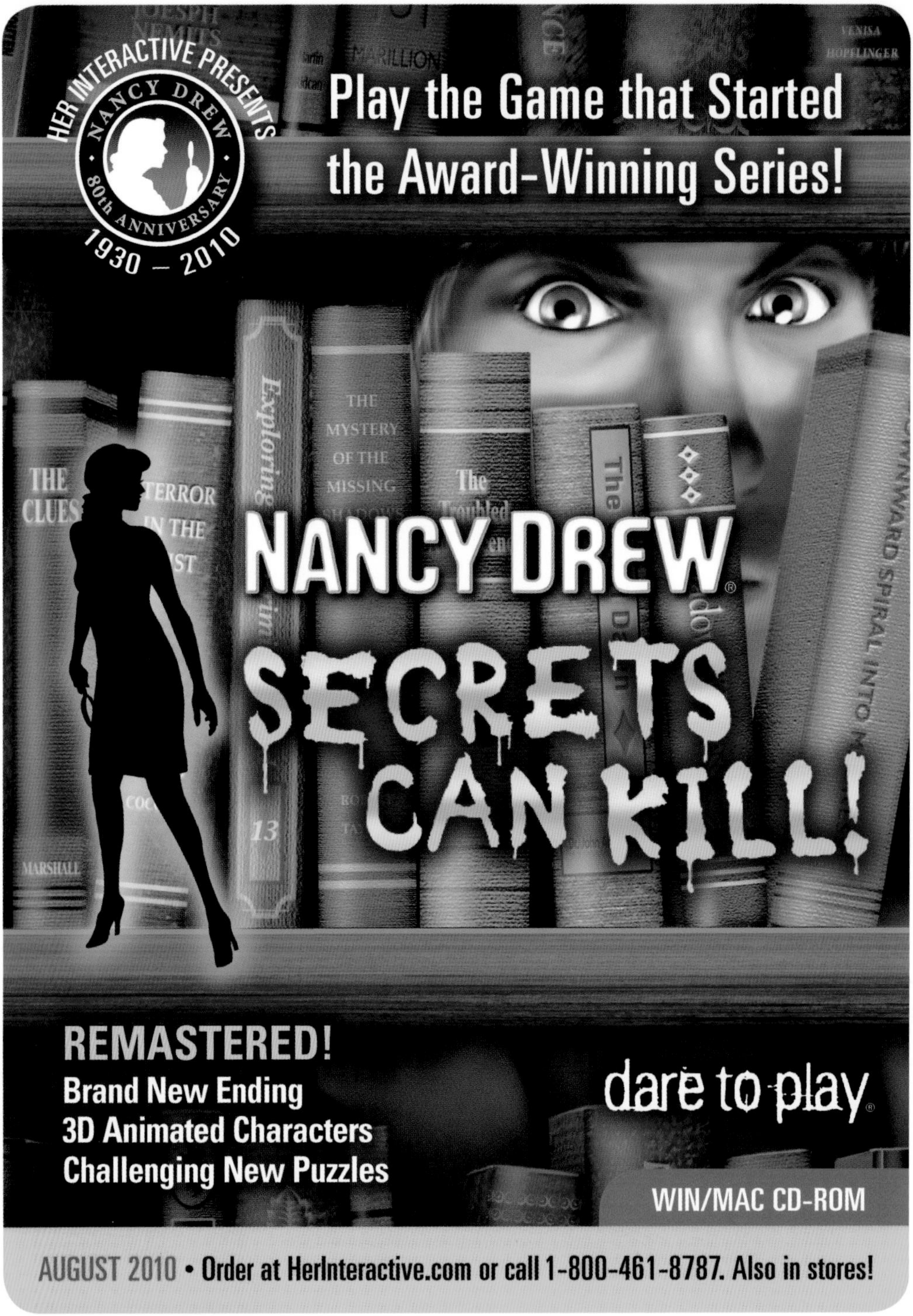

HER INTERACTIVE PRESENTS
NANCY DREW
80th ANNIVERSARY
1930 – 2010
Play the Game that Started the Award-Winning Series!
NANCY DREW®
SECRETS CAN KILL!
REMASTERED!
Brand New Ending
3D Animated Characters
Challenging New Puzzles
dare to play®
WIN/MAC CD-ROM
AUGUST 2010 • Order at HerInteractive.com or call 1-800-461-8787. Also in stores!

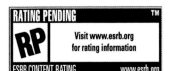